af
te r

t   h
                e
                a
                po
                ca
                ly
                ps e

after the apocalypse

stories

Maureen F. McHugh

Small Beer Press
Easthampton, MA

Small Beer Press
150 Pleasant Street #306
Easthampton, MA 01027
www.smallbeerpress.com
www.weightlessbooks.com
info@smallbeerpress.com

Distributed to the trade by Consortium.

Library of Congress Cataloging-in-Publication Data

McHugh, Maureen F.
After the apocalypse : stories / Maureen F. McHugh. -- 1st ed.
  p. cm.
ISBN 978-1-931520-29-4 (trade pbk. : alk. paper) -- ISBN 978-1-931520-35-5 (ebook)
i. Title.
PS3563.C3687A69 2011
813'.54--DC22

                          2011006769

First edition 1 2 3 4 5 6 7 8 9

Text set in Centaur 12 pt.

This book was printed on recycled paper in the USA.
Cover by TK.

Table of Contents

The Naturalist

Cahill lived in the Flats with about twenty other guys in a place that used to be an Irish bar called Fado. At the back of the bar was the Cuyahoga River, good for protection since zombies didn't cross the river. They didn't crumble into dust, they were just stupid as bricks, and they never built a boat or a bridge or built anything. Zombies were the ultimate trash. Worse than the guys who cooked meth in trailers. Worse than the fat women on WIC. Zombies were just useless dumbfucks.

"They're too dumb to find enough food to keep a stray cat going," Duck said.

Cahill was talking to a guy called Duck. Well, really, Duck was talking and Cahill was mostly listening. Duck had been speculating on the biology of zombies. He thought that the whole zombie thing was a virus, like Mad Cow Disease. A lot of the guys thought that. A lot of them mentioned that movie *28 Days Later,* where everybody but a few people had been driven crazy by a virus.

"But they gotta find something," Duck said. Duck had a prison tattoo of a mallard on his arm. Cahill wouldn't have known it was a mallard if Duck hadn't told him. He could just about tell it was a bird. Duck was over six feet tall, and Cahill would have hated to have been the guy who gave Duck such a shitty tattoo, 'cause Duck probably beat him senseless when he finally got a look at the thing. "Maybe," Duck mused, "maybe they're solar powered. And eating us is just a bonus."

"I think they go dormant when they don't smell us around," Cahill said.

Cahill didn't really like talking to Duck, but Duck often found Cahill and started talking to him. Cahill didn't know why. Most of the guys gave Duck a wide berth. Cahill figured it was probably easier to just talk to Duck when Duck wanted to talk.

Almost all of the guys at Fado were white. There was a Filipino guy, but he pretty much counted as white. As far as Cahill could tell there were two kinds of black guys, regular black guys and Nation of Islam. The Nation of Islam had gotten organized and turned a place across the street—a club called Heaven—into their headquarters. Most of the regular black guys lived below Heaven and in the building next door.

This whole area of the Flats had been bars and restaurants and clubs. Now it was a kind of compound with a wall of rubbish and dead cars forming a perimeter. Duck said that during the winter they had regular patrols organized by Whittaker and the Nation. Cold as shit standing behind a junked car on its side, watching for zombies. But they had killed off most of the zombies in this area, and now they didn't bother keeping watch. Occasionally a zombie wandered across the bridge and they had to take care of it, but in the time Cahill had been in Cleveland, he had seen exactly four zombies. One had been a woman.

Life in the zombie preserve really wasn't as bad as Cahill had expected. He'd been dumped off the bus and then spent a day skulking around expecting zombies to come boiling out of the floor like rats and eat him alive. He'd heard that the life expectancy of a guy in a preserve was something like two and a half days. But he'd only been here about a day and a half when he found a cache of liquor in the trunk of a car, and then some guys scavenging. He'd shown them where the liquor was, and they'd taken him back to the Flats.

Whittaker was a white guy who was sort of in charge. He'd made a big speech about how they were all more free here in the preserve than they'd ever been in a society that had no place for them, about how there used to be spaces for men with big appetites like the Wild West and Alaska—and how that was all gone now, but they were making a great space for themselves here in Cleveland, where they could live true to their own nature.

Cahill didn't think it was so great, and glancing around he was pretty sure that he wasn't the only one who wouldn't chuck the whole thing for a chance to sit and watch the Sox on TV. Bullshitting was what the Whittakers of the world did. It was part of running other people's lives. Cahill had dragged in a futon and made himself a little room. It had no windows and only one way in, which was good in case of attack. But he found most of the time he couldn't sleep there. A lot of times he slept outside on a picnic table someone had dragged out into the middle of the street.

What he really missed was carpet. He wanted to take a shower and then walk on carpet in a bedroom and get dressed in clean clothes.

A guy named Riley walked over to Cahill and Duck and said, "Hey, Cahill. Whittaker wants you to go scavenge."

Cahill hated to scavenge. It was nerve-wracking. It wasn't hard; there was a surprising amount left in the city, even after the groceries had been looted. He shrugged and thought about it and decided it was better not to say no to Whittaker. And it gave him an excuse to stop talking to Duck about zombies. He followed Riley and left Duck sitting looking at the water, enjoying the May sun.

"I think it's a government thing," Riley said. Riley was black but just regular black, not Nation of Islam. "I think it's a mutation of the AIDS virus."

Jesus Christ. "Yeah," Cahill said, hoping Riley would drop it.

"You know the whole AIDS thing was from the CIA, don't you? It was supposed to wipe out black people," Riley said.

"Then how come fags got it first?" Cahill asked.

He thought that might piss Riley off, but Riley seemed pleased to be able to explain how gay guys were the perfect way to introduce the disease because nobody cared fuckall what happened to them. But that really, fags getting it was an accident, because it was supposed to wipe out all the black people in Africa, and then the whites could just move into a whole new continent. Some queer stewardess got it in Africa and then brought it back here. It would kill white people, but it killed black people faster. And now if you were rich they could cure you, or at least give you drugs for your whole life so you wouldn't get sick and die, which was the same thing, but they were still letting black people and Africans die.

Cahill tuned Riley out. They collected two other guys. Riley was in charge. Cahill didn't know the names of the two other guys—a scrawny, white-trash, looking guy and a light-skinned black guy.

Riley quit talking once they had crossed the bridge and were in Cleveland.

On the blind, windowless side of a warehouse the wall had been painted white, and in huge letters it said:

Hell from beneath is moved for thee to meet thee at thy coming.
Isaiah (ch. XIV, v. 9)

This same quote was painted at the gate where the bus had dumped Cahill off.

There were crows gathering at Euclid, and, Riley guessed, maybe around East Ninth, so they headed north toward the lake. Zombies stank, and the crows tended to hang around them. Behind them the burned ruins of the Renaissance Hotel were still black and wet from the rain a couple of days ago.

When they saw the zombie, there were no crows, but that may have been because there was only one. Crows often meant a number of zombies. She fixed on them, turning her face toward them despite the blank whiteness of her eyes. She was black and her hair had once been in cornrows, though now half of it was loose and tangled. They all stopped and stood stock still. No one knew how zombies 'saw' people. Maybe infrared, like pit vipers. Maybe smell. Cahill could not tell from this far if she was sniffing. Or listening. Or maybe even tasting the air. Taste was one of the most primitive senses. Primitive as smell. Smelling with the tongue.

She went from standing there to loping toward them. That was one of the things about zombies. They didn't lean. They didn't anticipate. One minute they were standing there, the next minute they were running toward you. They didn't lead with their eyes or their chins. They were never surprised. They just were. As inexorable as rain. She didn't look as she ran, even though she was running through debris and rubble, placing her feet and sometimes barely leaping.

"Fuck," someone said.

"Pipes! Who's got pipes!" Riley shouted.

They all had pipes, and they all got them ready. Cahill wished he had a gun, but Whittaker confiscated guns. Hell, he wished he had an MK19, a grenade launcher. And a Humvee and some support, maybe with mortars, while he was at it.

Then she was on them, and they were all swinging like mad, because if she got her teeth into any of them, it was all over for that guy. The best thing to do was to keep up a goddamn flurry of swinging pipes so she couldn't get to anyone. Cahill hit other pipe, mostly, the impact clanging through his wrist bones, but sometimes when he hit the zombie he felt the melon thunk. She made no noise. No moaning, no hissing, no movie zombie noises, but even as they crushed her head and knocked her down (her eye socket gone soft and one eye a loose silken white sack) she kept moving and reaching. She didn't try to grab the pipes, she just reached for them until they had pounded her into broken bits.

She stank like old meat.

No blood. Which was strangely creepy. Cahill knew from experience that people had a lot more blood in them than you ever would have thought based on TV shows. Blood and blood and more blood. But this zombie didn't seem to have any blood.

Finally Riley yelled, "Get back, get back!" and they all stepped back.

All the bones in her arms and legs were broken, and her head was smashed to nothing. It was hard to tell she had ever looked like a person. The torso hitched its hips, raising its belly, trying to inchworm toward them, its broken limbs moving and shuddering like a seizure.

Riley shook his head and then said to them. "Anybody got any marks? Everybody strip."

Everybody stood there for a moment, ignoring him, watching the thing on the broken sidewalk.

Riley snarled, "I said strip, motherfuckers. Or nobody goes back to the compound."

"Fuck," one of the guys said, but they all did and, balls shriveled in the spring cold, paired off and checked each other for marks. When they each announced the other was clear, they all put their clothes back on and piled rubble on top of the twitching thing until they'd made a mound, while Riley kept an eye out for any others.

After that, everyone was pretty tense. They broke into an apartment complex above a storefront. The storefront had been looted and the windows looked empty as the socket of a pulled tooth, but the door to the apartments above was still locked, which meant that they might find stuff untouched. Cahill wondered: if zombies did go dormant without food, what if someone had gotten bit and gone back to this place, to their apartment? Could they be waiting for someone to enter the dark foyer, for the warmth and smell and the low steady big drum beat of the human heart to bring them back?

They went up the dark stairwell and busted open the door of the first apartment. It smelled closed, cold and dank. The furniture looked like it had been furnished from the curb, but it had a huge honking television. Which said everything about the guy who had lived here.

They ignored the TV. What they were looking for was canned goods. Chef Boy-ar-dee. Cans of beef stew. Beer. They all headed for the kitchen, and guys started flipping open cabinets.

Then, like a dumbshit, Cahill opened the refrigerator door. Even as he did it, he thought, "Dumbass."

The refrigerator had been full of food and then had sat, sealed and without power, while that food all rotted into a seething, shit-stinking mess. The smell was like a bomb. The inside was greenish black.

"Fuck!" someone said, and then they all got out of the kitchen. Cahill opened a window and stepped out onto the fire escape. It was closest, and everyone else was headed out into the living room where someone would probably take a swing at him for being an asshole. The fire escape was in an alley and he figured that he could probably get to the street and meet them in front, although he wasn't exactly sure how fire escapes worked.

Instead he froze. Below him, in the alley, there was one of those big dumpsters, painted green. The top was off the dumpster and inside it, curled up, was a zombie. Because it was curled up, he couldn't tell much about it—whether it was male or female, black or white. It looked small, and it was wearing a striped shirt.

The weird thing was that the entire inside of the dumpster had been covered in aluminum foil. There wasn't any sun yet in the alley but the dumpster was still a dull and crinkly mirror. As best he could tell, every bit was covered.

What the fuck was that about?

He waited for the zombie to sense him and raise its sightless face, but it didn't move. It was in one corner, like a gerbil or something in an aquarium. And all that freaking tinfoil. Had it gone into apartments and searched for aluminum foil? What for? To trap sun-light? Maybe Duck was right, they *were* solar powered. Or maybe it just liked shiny stuff.

The window had been hard to open, and it had been loud. He could still smell the reek of the kitchen. The sound and the stink should have alerted the zombie.

Maybe it was dead. Whatever that meant to a zombie.

He heard a distant *whump*. And then a couple more, with a dull rumble of explosion. It sounded like an air strike. The zombie stirred a little, not even raising its head. More like an animal disturbed in its sleep.

The hair was standing up on the back of Cahill's neck. From the zombie or the air strike, he couldn't tell. He didn't hear helicopters. He didn't hear anything. He stamped on the metal fire escape. It rang dully. The zombie didn't move.

He went back inside, through the kitchen and the now-empty apartment, down the dark stairwell. The other guys were standing around in the street, talking about the sounds they'd heard. Cahill didn't say anything, didn't say they were probably Hellfire missiles although they sure as hell sounded like them, and he didn't say there was a zombie in the alley. Nobody said anything to him about open-ing the refrigerator, which was fine by him.

Riley ordered them to head back to see what was up in the Flats.

While they were walking, the skinny little guy said, "Maybe one of those big cranes fell. You know, those big fuckers by the lake that they use for ore ships and shit."

Nobody answered.

"It could happen," the little guy insisted.

"Shut up," Riley said.

Cahill glanced behind them, unable to keep from checking his back. He'd been watching since they started moving, but the little zombie didn't seem to have woken up and followed them.

When they got to Public Square they could see the smoke rising, black and ugly, from the Flats.

"Fuck," Cahill said.

"What is that?" Riley said.

"Is that the camp?"

"Fuck is right."

"One of the buildings is on fire?"

Cahill wished they would shut the fuck up because he was listening for helicopters.

They headed for Main Avenue. By the time they got to West Tenth, there was a lot more smoke, and they could see some of it was rising from what used to be Shooters. They had to pick their way across debris. Fado and Heaven were gutted, the buildings blown out. Maybe someone was still alive. There were bodies. Cahill could see one in what looked like Whittaker's usual uniform of orange football jersey and black athletic shorts. Most of the head was missing.

"What the fuck?" Riley said.

"Air strike," Cahill said.

"Fuck that," Riley said. "Why would anyone do that?"

Because we weren't dying, Cahill thought. We weren't supposed to figure out how to stay alive. We certainly weren't supposed to establish some sort of base. Hell, the rats might get out of the cage.

The little guy who thought it might have been a crane walked up behind Riley and swung his pipe into the back of Riley's head. Riley staggered and the little guy swung again, and Riley's skull cracked audibly. They little guy hit a third time as Riley went down.

The little guy was breathing heavy. "Fucking bastard," he said, holding the pipe, glaring at them. "Whittaker's bitch."

Cahill glanced at the fourth guy with them. He looked as surprised as Cahill.

"You got a problem with this?" the little guy said.

Cahill wondered if the little guy had gotten scratched by the first zombie and they had missed it. Or if he was just bugfuck. Didn't matter. Cahill took a careful step back, holding his own pipe. And then another. The little guy didn't try to stop him.

He thought about waiting for a moment to see what the fourth guy would do. Two people would probably have a better chance than one. Someone to watch while the other slept. But the fourth guy was staring at the little guy and at Riley, who was laid out on the road, and he didn't seem to be able to wrap his head around the idea that their base was destroyed and Riley was dead.

Too stupid to live, and probably a liability. Cahill decided he was better off alone. Besides, Cahill had never really liked other people much anyway.

He found an expensive loft with a big white leather couch and a kitchen full of granite and stainless steel and a bed the size of a football field, and he stayed there for a couple of days, eating pouches of tuna he found next door, but it was too big and in a couple of days, the liquor cabinet was empty. By that time he had developed a deep and abiding hatred for the couple who had lived here. He had found pictures of them. A dark haired forty-ish guy with a kayak and a shit-eating grin. He had owned some kind of construction business. She was a toothy blonde with a big forehead who he mentally fucked every night in the big bed. It only made him crazy horny for actual sex.

He imagined they'd been evacuated. People like them didn't get killed, even when the zombies came. Even in the first panicked days when they were in dozens of cities and it seemed like the end of the world, before they'd gotten them under control. Somewhere they were sitting around in their new, lovely loft with working plumbing, telling their friends about how horrible it had been.

Finally, he dragged the big mattress to the freight elevator and then to the middle of the street out front. Long before he got it to the freight elevator, he had completely lost the righteous anger that had possessed him when he thought of the plan, but by then he was just pissed at everything. He considered torching the building but in the end he got the mattress down to the street, along with some pillows and cushions and magazines and kitchen chairs and set fire to the pile, then retreated to the third floor of the building across the way. Word was that zombies came for fire. Cahill was buzzing with a kind of suicidal craziness by this point, simultaneously terrified and elated. He settled in with a bottle of cranberry vodka, the last of the liquor from the loft, and a fancy martini glass, and waited. The vodka was not as awful as it sounded. The fire burned, almost transparent at first, and then orange and smoky.

After an hour he was bored and antsy. He jacked off with the picture of the toothy blonde. He drank more of the cranberry vodka. He glanced down at the fire, and they were there.

There were three of them, one standing by a light pole at the end of the street, one standing in the middle of the street, one almost directly below him. He grabbed his length of pipe and the baseball bat he'd found. He had been looking for a gun but hadn't found one. He wasn't sure that a gun would make much difference anyway. They were all unnaturally still. None of them had turned their blind faces toward him. They didn't seem to look at anything—not him, not the fire, not each other. They just stood there.

All of the shortcomings of this presented themselves. He had only one way out of the building, as far as he knew, and that was the door to the street where the zombies were. There was a back door, but someone had driven a UPS truck into it, and it was impassable. He didn't have any food. He didn't have much in the way of defense—he could have made traps. Found bedsprings and rigged up spikes so that if a zombie came in the hall and tripped it, it would slam the thing against the wall and shred it. Not that he had ever been particularly mechanical. He didn't really know how such a thing would work.

Lighter fluid. He could douse an area in lighter fluid or gasoline or something, and if a zombie came toward him, set fire to the fucker. Hell, even an idiot could make a Molotov cocktail.

All three of the zombies had once been men. One of them was so short he thought it was a child. Then he thought maybe it was a dwarf. One of them was wearing what might have once been a suit, which was a nice thing. Zombie businessmen struck Cahill as appropriate. The problem was that he didn't dare leave until they did, and the mattress looked ready to smolder for a good long time.

It did smolder for a good long time. The zombies just stood there, not looking at the fire, not looking at each other, not looking at anything. The zombie girl, the one they'd killed with Riley, she had turned her face in their direction. That was so far the most human thing he had seen a zombie do. He tried to see if their noses twitched or if they sniffed, but they were too far away. He added binoculars to his mental list of shit he hoped to find.

Eventually he went and explored some of the building he was in. It was offices, and the candy machine had been turned over and emptied. He worried when he prowled the darkened halls that the zombies had somehow sensed him, so he could only bring himself to explore for a few minutes at a time before he went back to his original window and checked. But they were just standing there. When it got dark, he wondered if they would lie down, maybe sleep like the one in the dumpster, but they didn't.

The night was horrible. There was no light in the city, of course. The street was dark enough that he couldn't see the short zombie. Where it was standing was a shadow, and a pretty much impenetrable one. The smoldering fire cast no real light at all. It was just an ashen heap that sometimes glowed red when a breeze picked up. Cahill nodded off and jerked awake, counting the zombies, wondering if the little one had moved in on him. If the short one sensed him, wouldn't they all sense him? Didn't the fact that two of them were still there mean that it was still there, too? It was hard to make out any of them, and sometimes he thought maybe they had all moved.

At dawn they were all three still there. All three still standing. Crows had gathered on the edge of the roof of a building down the street, probably drawn by the smell.

It sucked.

They stood there for that whole day, the night, and part of the next day before one of them turned and loped away, smooth as glass. The other two stood there for a while longer—an hour? He had no sense of time anymore. Then they moved off at the same time, not exactly together but apparently triggered by the same strange signal. He watched them lope off.

He made himself count slowly to one thousand. Then he did it again. Then finally he left the building.

For days the city was alive with zombies for him, although he didn't see any. He saw crows and avoided wherever he saw them. He headed for the lake and found a place not far from the Flats, an apartment over shops, with windows that opened. It wasn't near as swanky as the loft. He rigged up an alarm system that involved a bunch of thread crossing the open doorway to the stairwell and a bunch of wind chimes. Anything hit the thread and it would release the wind chimes which would fall and make enough noise to wake the fucking dead.

That night he slept for the first time since he had left the loft.

The next day he sat at the little kitchen table by the open window and wrote down everything he knew about zombies.

1. they stink
2. they can sense people
3. they didn't sense me because I was up above them? they couldn't smell me? they couldn't see me?

4. sometimes they sleep or something. sick? worn down? used up charge?
5. they like fire
6. they don't necessarily sleep
7. they like tinfoil???

Things he didn't know but wanted to:

1. do they eat animals
2. how do they sense people
3. how many are there
4. do they eventually die? fall apart? use up their energy?

It was somehow satisfying to have a list.

He decided to check out the zombie he had seen in the dumpster. He had a backpack now with water, a couple of cans of Campbell's Chunky soups—including his favorite, chicken and sausage gumbo, because if he got stuck somewhere like the last time, he figured he'd need something to look forward to—a tub of Duncan Hines Creamy Homestyle Chocolate Buttercream frosting for dessert, a can opener, a flashlight with batteries that worked, and his prize find, binoculars. Besides his length of pipe, he carried a Molotov cocktail: a wine bottle three-fourths filled with gasoline mixed with sugar, corked, with a gasoline-soaked rag rubber-banded to the top and covered with a sandwich bag so it wouldn't dry out.

He thought about cars as he walked. The trip he was making would take him an hour, and it would have been five minutes in a car. People in cars had no fucking appreciation for how big places were. Nobody would be fat if there weren't any cars. Far down the street, someone came out of a looted store carrying a cardboard box.

Cahill stopped and then dropped behind a pile of debris from a sandwich shop. If it was a zombie, he wasn't sure hiding wouldn't make any difference, and he pulled his lighter out of his pocket, ready to throw the bottle. But it wasn't a zombie. Zombies, as far as he knew, didn't carry boxes of loot around. The guy with the box must have seen Cahill moving, because he dropped the box and ran.

Cahill occasionally saw other convicts, but he avoided them, and so far, they avoided him. There was a one dude who Cahill was pretty sure lived somewhere around the wreckage of the Renaissance Hotel. He didn't seem to want any company, either. Cahill followed to where this new guy had disappeared around a corner. The guy was watching, and when he saw Cahill, he jogged away, watching over his shoulder to see if Cahill would follow. Cahill stood until the guy had turned the corner.

By the time Cahill got to the apartment where he'd seen the zombie in the dumpster, he was pretty sure that the other guy had gotten behind him and was following him. It irritated him. Dickweed. He thought about not going upstairs but decided that since the guy wasn't in sight at the moment, it would give Cahill a chance to disappear. Besides, they hadn't actually checked out the apartment, and there might be something worth scavenging. In Cahill's months of scavenging, he had never seen a zombie in an apartment, or even any evidence of one, but he always checked carefully. The place was empty, still stinking a little of the contents of the fridge, but the smell was no worse than a lot of places and a lot better than some. Rain had come in where he'd left the kitchen window open, warping the linoleum. He climbed out onto the fire escape and looked down. The dumpster was empty, although still lined with some tattered aluminum foil. He pulled out his binoculars and checked carefully, but he couldn't really see anything.

He stood for a long time. Truthfully he couldn't be a hundred percent sure it was a zombie. Maybe it had been a child, some sort of refugee? Hard to imagine any child surviving in the city. No, it had to be a zombie. He considered lighting and tossing the Molotov cocktail and seeing if the zombie came to the alley, but he didn't want to wait it out in this apartment building. Something about this place made him feel vulnerable.

Eventually he rummaged through the apartment. The bedside table held neither handgun nor D batteries, two things high on his scavenger list. He went back down the dark stairwell and stopped well back from the doorway. Out in the middle of the street, in front of the building to his left but visible from where he stood, was an offering. A box with a bottle of whiskey set on it. Like some kind of perverse lemonade stand.

Fucking dickweed.

If the guy had found a handgun, he could be waiting in ambush. Cahill figured there was a good chance he could outlast the guy, but he hated waiting in the stairwell. There were no apartments on the first level, just a hallway between two storefronts. Cahill headed back upstairs. The apartment he'd been in before didn't look out the front of the building. The one that did was locked.

Fuck.

Breaking open the lock would undoubtedly make a hell of a lot of racket. He went back to the first apartment, checked one more time for the zombie, and peed in the empty toilet. He grabbed a pillow from the bed.

Cahill went back downstairs and sat down on the bottom step and wedged the pillow in behind his back. He set up his bottle and his lighter beside him on the step, and his pipe on the other side, and settled in to watch. He could at least wait until dark, although it wasn't even mid-morning yet. After a while he ate his soup—the can opener sounded louder than it probably was.

It was warm midday and Cahill was drowsy warm when the guy finally, nervously, walked out to the box and picked up the whiskey. Cahill sat still in the shadow of the stairwell with his hand on his pipe. As best as he could tell, he was unnoticed. The guy was a tall, skinny black man wearing a brown Cleveland football jersey and a pair of expensive looking, olive-green suit pants. Cahill looked out and watched the guy walk back up the street. After a minute, Cahill followed.

When Cahill got out to the main drag, the guy was walking up Superior toward the center of downtown. Cahill took a firm hold of his pipe.

"Hey," he said. His voice carried well in the silence.

The guy started and whirled around.

"What the fuck you want?" Cahill asked.

"Bro," the man said. "Hey, were you hiding back there?" He laughed nervously and held up the bottle. "Peace offering, bro. Just looking to make some peace."

"What do you want?" Cahill asked.

"Just, you know, wanna talk. Talk to someone who knows the ropes, you know? I just got here and I don't know what the fuck is going on, bro."

"This is a fucking penal colony," Cahill said.

"Yeah," the guy laughed. "A fucking zombie preserve. I been watching out for them zombies. You look like you been here awhile."

Cahill hadn't bothered to shave, and last time he'd glanced in a mirror he'd looked like Charles Manson, only taller. "Lie down with your hands away from your body," Cahill said.

The black guy squinted at Cahill. "You shittin' me."

"How do I know you don't have a gun?" Cahill asked.

"Bro, I don't got no gun. I don't got nothin' but what you see." Cahill waited.

"Listen, I'm just trying to be friendly," the guy said. "I swear to God, I don't have anything. How do I know *you're* not going to do something to me? You're a freaky dude—you know that?"

The guy talked for about five minutes, finally talking himself into lying down on his stomach with his arms out. Cahill moved fast, patting him down. The guy wasn't lying: he didn't have anything on him.

"Fuck man," the guy said. "I told you that." Once he was sure Cahill wasn't going to do anything to him, he talked even more. His name was LaJon Watson, and his lawyer had told him there was no way they were going to drop him in the Cleveland Zombie Preserve, because the Supreme Court was going to declare it unconstitutional. His lawyer had been saying that right up until the day they put LaJon on the bus, which was when LaJon realized that his lawyer knew shit. LaJon wanted to know if Cahill had seen any zombies and what they were like and how Cahill had stayed alive.

Cahill found it hard to talk. He hadn't talked to anyone in weeks. Usually someone like LaJon Watson would have driven him nuts, but it was nice to let the tide of talk wash over him while they walked. He wasn't sure that he wouldn't regret it, but he took LaJon back to his place. LaJon admired his alarm system. "You gotta show me how to unhook it and hook it back up. Don't they see it? I mean, has one of them ever hit it?"

"No," Cahill said. "I don't think they can see."

There were scientists studying zombies, and sometimes there was zombie stuff on Fox News, but LaJon said he hadn't paid much attention to all that. He really hadn't expected to need to know about zombies. In fact, he hadn't been sure at first that Cahill wasn't a zombie. Cahill opened cans of Campbell's Chunky Chicken and Dumplings. LaJon asked if Cahill warmed them over a fire or what. Cahill handed him a can and a spoon.

LaJon wolfed down the soup. LaJon wouldn't shut up, even while eating. He told Cahill how he'd looked in a bunch of shops, but most of them had been pretty thoroughly looted. He'd looked in an apartment, but the only thing on the shelves in a can was tomato paste and evaporated milk. Although now that he thought about it, maybe he could have made some sort of tomato soup or something. He hadn't slept in the two days he'd been here, and he was going crazy, and it was a great fucking thing to have found somebody who could show him the ropes.

LaJon was from Cincinnati. Did Cahill know anybody from Cincinnati? Where had Cahill been doing time? (Auburn.) LaJon didn't know anybody at Auburn, wasn't that New York? LaJon had been at Lebanon Correctional. Cahill was a nice dude, if quiet. Who else was around, and was there anyone LaJon could score from? (Cahill said he didn't know.) What did people use for money here anyway?

"I been thinking," LaJon said, "about the zombies. I think it's pollution that's mutating them like the Teenage Mutant Ninja Turtles."

Cahill decided it had been a mistake to bring LaJon. He picked up the bottle of whiskey and opened it. He didn't usually use glasses but got two out of the cupboard and poured them each some whiskey.

LaJon apologized, "I don't usually talk this much," he said. "I guess I just fucking figured I was dead when they dropped me here." He took a big drink of whiskey. "It's like my mouth can't stop."

Cahill poured LaJon more to drink and nursed his own whiskey. Exhaustion and nerves were telling: LaJon was finally slowing down. "You want some frosting?" Cahill asked.

Frosting and whiskey was a better combination than it had any right to be. Particularly for a man who'd thought himself dead. LaJon nodded off.

"Come on," Cahill said. "It's going to get stuffy in here." He got the sleepy drunk up on his feet.

"What?" LaJon said.

"I sleep outside, where it's cooler." It was true that the apartment got hot during the day.

"Bro, there's zombies out there," LaJon mumbled.

"It's okay, I've got a system," Cahill said. "I'll get you downstairs, and then I'll bring down something to sleep on."

LaJon wanted to sleep where he was and, for a moment, his eyes narrowed to slits and something scary was in his face.

"I'm going to be there, too," Cahill said. "I wouldn't do anything to put myself in danger."

LaJon allowed himself to be half-carried downstairs. Cahill was worried when he had to unhook the alarm system. He propped LaJon up against the wall and told him, 'Just a moment.' If LaJon slid down the wall and passed out, he'd be hell to get downstairs. But the lanky black guy stood there long enough for Cahill to get the alarm stuff out of the way. He was starting to sober up a little. Cahill got him down to the street.

"I'll get the rest of the whiskey," Cahill said.

"What the fuck you playing at?" LaJon muttered.

Cahill took the stairs two at a time in the dark. He grabbed pillows, blankets, and the whiskey bottle and went back down to the sidewalk. He handed LaJon the whiskey bottle. "It's not so hot out here," he said, although it was on the sidewalk with the sunlight.

LaJon eyed him drunkenly.

Cahill went back upstairs and came down with a bunch of couch cushions. He made a kind of bed and got LaJon to sit on it. "We're okay in the day," he said. "Zombies don't like the light. I sleep in the day. I'll get us upstairs before night."

LaJon shook his head, took another slug of whiskey, and lay back on the cushions. "I feel sick," he said.

Cahill thought the motherfucker was going to throw up, but instead LaJon was snoring.

Cahill sat for a bit, planning and watching the street. After a bit, he went back to his apartment. When he found something good scavenging, he squirreled it away. He came downstairs with duct tape. He taped LaJon's ankles together. Then his wrists. Then he sat LaJon up. LaJon opened his eyes, said, "What the fuck?" drunkenly. Cahill taped LaJon's arms to his sides, right at his elbows, running the tape all the way around his torso. LaJon started to struggle, but Cahill was methodical and patient, and he used the whole roll of tape to secure LaJon's arms. From shoulders to waist, LaJon was a duct tape mummy.

LaJon swore at him, colorfully, then monotonously.

Cahill left him there and went looking. He found an upright dolly at a bar and brought it back. It didn't do so well where the pavement was uneven, but he didn't think he could carry LaJon far, and if he was going to build a fire, he didn't want it to be close to his place, where zombies could pin him in his apartment. LaJon was still where he had left him, although when he saw Cahill, he went into a frenzy of struggling. Cahill let him struggle. He lay the dolly down and rolled LaJon onto it. LaJon fought like anything, so in the end, Cahill went back upstairs and got another roll of duct tape and duct-taped LaJon to the dolly. That was harder than duct-taping LaJon the first time, because LaJon was scared and pissed now. When Cahill finally pulled the dolly up, LaJon struggled so hard that the dolly was unmanageable, which pissed Cahill off so much he just let go.

LaJon went over and without hands to stop himself, face-planted on the sidewalk. That stilled him. Cahill pulled the dolly upright then. LaJon's face was a bloody mess, and it looked like he might have broken a couple of teeth. He was conscious, but stunned. Cahill started pushing the dolly, and LaJon threw up.

It took a couple of hours to get six blocks. LaJon was sober and silent by the time Cahill decided he'd gone far enough.

Cahill sat down, sweating, and used his T-shirt to wipe his face.

"You a bug," LaJon said.

Bug was prison slang for someone crazy. LaJon said it with certainty.

"Just my fucking luck. Kind of luck I had all my life. I find one guy alive in this fucking place, and he a bug." LaJon spat. "What are you gonna do to me?"

Cahill was so tired of LaJon that he considered going back to his place and leaving LaJon here. Instead, he found a door and pried it open with a tire iron. It had been an office building, and the second floor was fronted with glass. He had a hell of a time finding a set of service stairs that opened from the outside on the first floor. He found some chairs and dragged them downstairs. Then he emptied file cabinets, piling the papers around the chairs. LaJon watched him, getting more anxious.

When it looked like he'd get a decent fire going, he put LaJon next to it. The blood had dried on LaJon's face and he'd bruised up a bit. It was evening.

Cahill set fire to the papers and stood, waiting for them to catch. Burnt paper drifted up, raised by the fire.

LaJon squinted at the fire, then at Cahill. "You gonna burn me?"

Cahill went in the building and settled upstairs where he could watch.

LaJon must have figured that Cahill wasn't going to burn him. Then he began to worry about zombies. Cahill watched him start twisting around, trying to look around. The dolly rocked and LaJon realized that if he wasn't careful, the dolly would go over again and he'd faceplant and not be able to see.

Cahill gambled that the zombies wouldn't be there right away, and he found a soda machine in the hallway. He broke it open with his tire iron and got himself a couple of Cokes and then went back to watch it get dark. The zombies weren't there yet. He opened a warm Coke and settled in a desk chair from one of the offices—much more comfortable than the cubicle chairs. He opened a jar of peanut butter and ate it with a spoon.

It came so fast that he didn't see it until it was at the fire. LaJon saw it before he did and went rigid with fear. The fire was between LaJon and the zombie.

It just stood there, not watching the fire, but standing there. Not 'looking' at LaJon, either. Cahill leaned forward. He tried to read its body language. It had been a man, overweight, maybe middle-aged, but now it was predatory and gracile. It didn't seem to do any normal things. It was moving, and it stopped. Once stopped, it was still. An object rather than an animal. Like the ones that had come to the mattress fire, it didn't seem to need to shift its weight. After a few minutes, another one came from the same direction and stopped, looking at the fire. It had once been a man, too. It still wore glasses. Would there be a third? Did they come in threes? Cahill imagined a zombie family. Little triplets of zombies, all apparently oblivious of each other. Maybe the zombie he'd seen was still in the zombie den? He had never figured out where the zombies stayed.

LaJon was still and silent with terror, but the zombies didn't seem to know or care that he was there. They just stood, slightly askew and indifferent. Was it the fire? Would they notice LaJon when the fire died down?

Then there was a third one, but it came from the other side of the fire, the same side LaJon was on, so there was no fire between it and LaJon. Cahill saw it before LaJon did, and from its directed lope he was sure it was aware of LaJon. LaJon saw it just before it got to him. His mouth opened wide and it was on him, hands and teeth. LaJon was clearly screaming, although behind the glass of the office building, Cahill couldn't hear him.

Cahill was watching the other zombies. They didn't react to the noise at all. Even when there was blood all over, they didn't seem to sense anything. Cahill reflected, not for the first time, that it actually took people a lot longer to die than it did on television or in the movies. He noted that the one that had mauled and eventually killed LaJon did not seem to prefer brains. Sometime in the night, the fire died down enough that the zombies on the wrong side of the fire seemed to sense the body of LaJon, and in an instant, they were feeding. The first one, apparently sated, just stood, indifferent. Two more showed up in the hours before dawn and fed in the dim red of the embers of the fire. When they finally left, almost two days later, there was nothing but broken bones and scattered teeth.

Cahill lay low for a while after that, feeling exhausted. It was hot during the day, and the empty city baked. But after a few days, he went out and found another perch and lit another fire. Four zombies came to that fire, despite the fact that it was smaller than his first two. They had all been women. He still had his picture of the toothy blonde from the loft, and after masturbating, he looked out at the zombie women, blank-white eyes and indifferent bodies, and wondered if the toothy blonde had been evacuated or if she might show up at one of his fires. None of the women at the fire appeared to be her, although it wasn't always easy to tell. One was clearly wearing the remnants of office clothes, but the other three were blue-jean types and all four had such rat's nests of hair that he wasn't sure if their hair was short or long.

A couple of times he encountered zombies while scavenging. Both times his Molotov cocktails worked, catching fire. He didn't set the zombies on fire, just threw the bottle so that the fire was between him and the zombie. He watched them stop, then he backed away, fast. He set up another blind in an apartment and, over the course of a week, built a scaffolding and a kind of block-and-tackle arrangement. Then he started hanging around where the bus dropped people off, far enough back that the guys patrolling the gate didn't start shooting or something. He'd scoured up some bottles of water and used them to shave and clean up a bit.

When they dropped a new guy off, Cahill trailed him for half a day and then called out and introduced himself. The new guy was an Aryan Nation asshole named Jordan Schmidtzinsky who was distrustful but willing to be led back to Cahill's blind. He wouldn't get drunk, though, and in the end, Cahill had to brain him with a pipe. Still, it was easier to tape up the unconscious Schmidtzinsky than it had been the conscious LaJon. Cahill hoisted him into the air, put a chair underneath him so a zombie could reach him, and then set the fire.

Zombies did not look up. Schmidtzinsky dangled above the zombies for two whole days. Sometime in there he died. They left without ever noticing him. Cahill cut him down and lit another fire and discovered that zombies were willing to eat the dead, although they had to practically fall over the body to find it.

Cahill changed his rig so he could lower the bait. The third guy was almost Cahill's undoing. Cahill let him wander for two days in the early autumn chill before appearing and offering to help. This guy, a black city kid from Nashville who for some reason wouldn't say his name, evidently didn't like the scaffolding outside. He wouldn't take any of Cahill's whiskey, and when Cahill pretended to sleep, the guy made the first move. Cahill was lucky not to get killed, managing again to brain the guy with his pipe.

But it was worth it, because when he suspended the guy and lit the fire, one of the four zombies that showed up was the skinny guy who'd killed Riley back the day the air strike had wiped out the camp.

He was white-eyed like the other zombies, but still recognizable. It made Cahill feel even more that the toothy blonde might be out there, unlikely as that actually was. Cahill watched for a couple of hours before he lowered Nashville. The semiconscious Nashville started thrashing and making weird coughing, choking noises as soon as Cahill pulled on the rope, but the zombies were oblivious. Cahill was gratified to see that once the semiconscious Nashville got about so his shoes were about four feet above the ground, three of four zombies around the fire (the ones for whom the fire was not between them and Nashville) turned as one and swarmed up the chair.

He was a little nervous that they would look up—he had a whole plan for how he would get out of the building—but he didn't have to use it.

The three zombies ate, indifferent to each other and the fourth zombie, and then stood.

Cahill entertained himself with thoughts of the toothy blonde and then dozed. The air was crisp, but Cahill was warm in an overcoat. The fire smelled good. He was going to have to think about how he was going to get through the winter without a fire—unless he could figure out a way to keep a fire going well above the street and above zombie attention, but right now things were going okay.

He opened his eyes and saw one of the zombies bob its head.

He'd never seen that before. Jesus, did that mean it was aware? That it might come upstairs? He had his length of pipe in one hand and a Molotov in the other. The zombies were all still. A long five minutes later, the zombie did it again, a quick, birdlike head bob. Then, bob-bob, twice more, and on the second bob, the other two that had fed did it, too. They were still standing there, faces turned just slightly different directions as if they were unaware of each other, but he had seen it.

Bob-bob-bob. They all three did it. All at the same time.

Every couple of minutes they'd do it again. It was—communal. Animal-like. They did it for a couple of hours, and then they stopped. The one on the other side of the fire never did it at all. The fire burned low enough that the fourth one came over and worked on the remnants of the corpse, and the first three just stood there.

Cahill didn't know what the fuck they were doing, but it made him strangely happy.

When they came to evacuate him, Cahill thought at first it was another air strike operation—a mopping up. He'd been sick for a few days, throwing up, something he ate, he figured. He was scavenging in a looted drug store, hoping for something to take—although everything was gone or ruined—when he heard the patrol coming. They weren't loud, but in the silent city noise was exaggerated. He had looked out of the shop, seen the patrol of soldiers, and tried to hide in the dark ruins of the pharmacy.

"Come on out," the patrol leader said. "We're here to get you out of this place."

Bullshit, Cahill thought. He stayed put.

"I don't want to smoke you out, and I don't want to send guys in there after you," the patrol leader said. "I've got tear gas, but I really don't want to use it."

Cahill weighed his options. He was fucked either way. He tried to go out the back of the pharmacy, but they had already sent someone around, and he was met by two scared nineteen-year-olds with guns. He figured the writing was on the wall and put his hands up.

But the weird twist was that they *were* evacuating him. There'd been some big government scandal. The Supreme Court had closed the reserves, the president had been impeached, elections were coming. He wouldn't find that out for days. What he found out right then was that they hustled him back to the gate, and he walked out past rows of soldiers into a wall of noise and light. Television cameras showed him lost and blinking in the glare.

"What's your name?"

"Gerrold Cahill," he said.

"Hey, Gerrold! Look over here!" a hundred voices called.

It was overwhelming. They all called out at the same time, and it was mostly just noise to him, but if he could understand a question, he tried to answer it. "How's it feel to be out of there?"

"Loud," he said. "And bright."

"What do you want to do?"

"Take a hot shower and eat some hot food."

There was a row of sawhorses, and the cameras and lights were all behind them. A guy with corporal's stripes was trying to urge him toward a trailer, but Cahill was like someone knocked down by a wave who tries to get to his feet only to be knocked down again.

"Where are you from?" "Tell us what it was like!"

"What was it like?" Cahill said. Dumbshit question. What was he supposed to say to that? But his response had had the marvelous effect of quieting them for a moment, which allowed him to maybe get his bearings a little. "It wasn't so bad."

The barrage started again, but he picked out, "Were you alone?"

"Except for the zombies."

They liked that, and the surge was almost animalistic. Had he seen zombies? How had he survived? He shrugged and grinned.

"Are you glad to be going back to prison?"

He had an answer for that, one he didn't even know was in him. He would repeat it in the interview he gave to the *Today Show* and again in the interview for *20/20*. "Cleveland was better than prison," he said. "No alliances, no gangs, just zombies."

Someone called, "Are you glad they're going to eradicate the zombies?"

"They're going to what?" he asked.

The barrage started again, but he said, "What are they going to do to the zombies?"

"They're going to eradicate them, like they did everywhere else."

"Why?" he asked.

This puzzled the mob. "Don't you think they should be?"

He shook his head.

"Gerrold! Why not?"

Why not indeed? "Because," he said, slowly, and the silence came down, except for the clicking of cameras and the hum of the news vans idling, "because they're just ... like animals. They're just doing what's in their nature to be doing." He shrugged.

Then the barrage started again. "Gerrold! Gerrold! Do you think people are evil?" But by then he was on his way to a military trailer, an examination by an army doctor, a cup of hot coffee, and a meal and a long hot shower.

Behind him the city was dark. At the moment, it felt cold behind him, but safe, too, in its quiet. He didn't really want to go back there. Not yet.

He wished he'd had time to set them one last fire before he'd left.

Special Economics

W hat are you doing?" a guy asked her.
"I am divorced," she said. She had always thought of
herself as a person who would one day be divorced, so
it didn't seem like a big stretch to claim it. Staying married to one
person was boring. She figured she was too complicated for that.
Interesting people had complicated lives. "I'm looking for a job. But
I do hip-hop, too" she explained.

"Hip-hop?" He was a middle-aged man with stubble on his chin
who looked as if he wasn't looking for a job but should be.

"Not like Shanghai," she said, "Not like Hi-Bomb. They do
gangsta stuff, which I don't like. Old fashioned. Like M.I.A.," she
said. "Except not political, of course." She gave a big smile. This
was all way beyond the guy. Jieling started the boom box. M.I.A was
Maya Arulpragasam, a Sri Lankan hip-hop artist who had started all
on her own years ago. She had sung, she had danced, she had done
her own videos. Of course M.I.A. lived in London, which made it
easier to do hip-hop and become famous.

Jieling had no illusions about being a hip-hop singer, but it had
been a good way to make some cash up north in Baoding where she
came from. Set up in a plague-trash market and dance for yuan.

Jieling did her opening, her own hip-hop moves, a little like
Maya and a little like some things she had seen on MTV, but not too
sexy, because Chinese people did not throw you money if you were

too sexy. Only April, and it was already hot and humid.
  Ge down, ge down,
  lang-a-lang-a-lang-a.
  Ge down, ge down,
  lang-a-lang-a-lang-a.

She had borrowed the English. It sounded very fresh. Very criminal.
  The guy said, "How old are you?"
  "Twenty-two," she said, adding three years to her age, still dancing and singing.
  Maybe she should have told him she was a widow? Or an orphan?
But there were too many orphans and widows after so many people
died in the bird flu plague. There was no margin in that. Better to be
divorced. He didn't throw any money at her, just flicked open his cellphone to check listings from the market for plague trash. This plague-
trash market was so big it was easier to check online, even if you were
standing right in the middle of it. She needed a new cell phone. Hers
had finally fallen apart right before she headed south.
  Shenzhen people were apparently too jaded for hip-hop. She
made fifty-two yuan, which would pay for one night in a bad hotel
where country people washed cabbage in the communal sink.
  The market was full of secondhand stuff. When over a quarter
of a billion people died in four years, there was a lot of second-hand
stuff. But there was still a part of the market for new stuff and street
food, and that's where Jieling found the cell phone seller. He had a
cart with stacks of flat plastic cell phone kits printed with circuits and
scored. She flipped through; tiger-striped, peonies (old lady phones)
metallics (old man phones), anime characters, moon phones, expensive lantern phones. "Where is your printer?" she asked.
  "At home," he said. "I print them up at home, bring them here.
No electricity here." Up north in Baoding she'd always bought them

in a store where they let you pick your pattern online and then printed them there. More to pick from.

On the other hand, he had a whole box full of ones that hadn't sold that he would let go for cheap. In the stack she found a purple one with kittens that wasn't too bad. Very Japanese, which was also very fresh this year. And only one hundred yuan for phone and three hundred minutes.

He took the flat plastic sheet from her and dropped it in a pot of boiling water big enough to make dumplings. The hinges embedded in the sheet were made of plastic with molecular memory and when they got hot, they bent, and the plastic folded into a rough cell phone shape. He fished the phone out of the water with tongs, let it sit for a moment, and then pushed all the seams together so they snapped. "Wait about an hour for it to dry before you use it," he said and handed her the warm phone.

"An *hour*," she said. "I need it now. I need a job."

He shrugged. "Probably okay in half an hour," he said.

She bought a newspaper and scallion pancake from a street food vendor, sat on a curb, and ate while her phone dried. The paper had some job listings, but it also had a lot of listings from recruiters. ONE MONTH BONUS PAY! BEST JOBS! and NUMBER ONE JOBS! START BONUS! People scowled at her for sitting on the curb. She looked like a farmer, but what else was she supposed to do? She checked listings on her new cell phone. Online there were a lot more listings than in the paper. It was a good sign. She picked one at random and called.

The woman at the recruiting office was a flat-faced southerner with buckteeth. Watermelon-picking teeth. But she had a manicure and a very nice red suit. The office was not so nice. It was small, and the furniture was old. Jieling was groggy from a night spent at a hotel on the edge of the city. It had been cheap but very loud.

The woman was very sharp in the way she talked and had a strong accent that made it hard to understand her. Maybe Fujian, but Jieling wasn't sure. The recruiter had Jieling fill out an application.

"Why did you leave home?" the recruiter asked.

"To get a good job," Jieling said.

"What about your family? Are they alive?"

"My mother is alive. She is remarried," Jieling said. "I wrote it down."

The recruiter pursed her lips. "I can get you an interview on Friday," she said.

"Friday!" Jieling said. It was Tuesday. She had only three hundred yuan left out of the money she had brought. "But I need a job!"

The recruiter looked sideways at her. "You have made a big gamble to come to Shenzhen."

"I can go to another recruiter," Jieling said.

The recruiter tapped her lacquered nails. "They will tell you the same thing," she said.

Jieling reached down to pick up her bag.

"Wait," the recruiter said. "I do know of a job. But they only want girls of very good character."

Jieling put her bag down and looked at the floor. Her character was fine. She was not a loose girl, whatever this woman with her big front teeth thought.

"Your Mandarin is very good. You say you graduated with high marks from high school," the recruiter said.

"I liked school," Jieling said, which was only partly not true. Everybody here had terrible Mandarin. They all had thick southern accents. Lots of people spoke Cantonese in the street.

"Okay. I will send you to ShinChi for an interview. I cannot get you an interview before tomorrow. But you come here at 8:00 a.m. and I will take you over there."

ShinChi. New Life. It sounded very promising. "Thank you," Jieling said. "Thank you very much."

But outside in the heat, she counted her money and felt a creeping fear. She called her mother.

Her stepfather answered, "*Wei.*"

"Is Ma there?" she asked.

"Jieling!" he said. "Where are you!"

"I'm in Shenzhen," she said, instantly impatient with him. "I have a job here."

"A job! When are you coming home?"

He was always nice to her. He meant well. But he drove her nuts. "Let me talk to Ma," she said.

"She's not here," her stepfather said. "I have her phone at work. But she's not home, either. She went to Beijing last weekend, and she's shopping for fabric now."

Her mother had a little tailoring business. She went to Beijing every few months and looked at clothes in all the good stores. She didn't buy in Beijing; she just remembered. Then she came home, bought fabric, and sewed copies. Jieling's stepfather had been born in Beijing and she thought that was part of the reason her mother had married him. He was more like her mother than her father had been. There was nothing in particular wrong with him. He just set her teeth on edge.

"I'll call back later," Jieling said.

"Wait, your number is blocked," her stepfather said. "Give me your number."

"I don't even know it yet," Jieling said and hung up.

The New Life company was a huge, modern-looking building with a lot of windows. Inside it was full of reflective surfaces and very clean. Sounds echoed in the lobby. A man in a very smart gray suit met Jieling and the recruiter, and the recruiter's red suit looked cheaper, her glossy fingernails too red, her buckteeth exceedingly large. The man in the smart gray suit was short and slim and very southern looking. Very city.

Jieling took some tests on her math and her written characters and got good scores.

To the recruiter, the human resources man said, "Thank you, we will send you your fee." To Jieling he said, "We can start you on Monday."

"Monday?" Jieling said. "But I need a job now!" He looked grave. "I ... I came from Baoding, in Hebei," Jieling explained. "I'm staying in a hotel, but I don't have much money."

The human resources man nodded. "We can put you up in our guesthouse," he said. "We can deduct the money from your wages when you start. It's very nice. It has television and air conditioning, and you can eat in the restaurant."

It was very nice. There were two beds. Jieling put her backpack on the one nearest the door. There was carpeting, and the windows were covered in gold drapes with a pattern of cranes flying across them. The television got stations from Hong Kong. Jieling didn't understand the Cantonese, but there was a button on the remote for subtitles. The movies had lots of violence and more sex than mainland movies did— like the bootleg American movies for sale in the market. She wondered how much this room was. Two hundred yuan? Three hundred yuan?

Jieling watched movies the whole first day, one right after another.

On Monday she began orientation. She was given two pale green uniforms, smocks and pants like medical people wore and little caps and two pairs of white shoes. In the uniform she looked a little like a model worker—which is to say that the clothes were not sexy and made her look fat. There were two other girls in their green uniforms. They all watched a DVD about the company.

New Life did biotechnology. At other plants they made influenza vaccine (on the screen were banks and banks of chicken eggs), but at this plant they were developing breakthrough technologies in tissue culture. It showed many men in suits. Then it showed a big American store and explained how they were forging new exportation ties with the biggest American corporation for selling goods, Wal-Mart. It also showed a little bit of an American movie about Wal-Mart. Subtitles explained how Wal-Mart was working with companies around the world to improve living standards, decrease CO_2 emissions, and give people low prices. The voice narrating the DVD never really explained the breakthrough technologies.

One of the girls was from way up north; she had a strong Northern way of talking.

"How long are you going to work here?" the northern girl asked. She looked as if she might even have some Russian in her.

"How long?" Jieling said.

"I'm getting married," the northern girl confided. "As soon as I make enough money, I'm going home. If I haven't made enough money in a year," the northern girl explained, "I'm going home anyway."

Jieling hadn't really thought she would work here long. She didn't know exactly what she would do, but she figured that a big city like Shenzhen was a good place to find out. This girl's plans seemed very ... country. No wonder Southern Chinese thought Northerners had to wipe the pig shit off their feet before they got on the train.

"Are you Russian?" Jieling asked.

"No," said the girl. "I'm Manchu."

"Ah," Jieling said. Manchu like Manchurian. Ethnic Minority. Jieling had gone to school with a boy who was classified as Manchu, which meant that he was allowed to have two children when he got married. But he had looked Han Chinese like everyone else. This girl had the hook nose and the dark skin of a Manchu. Manchu used to rule China until the Communist Revolution (there was something in-between with Sun Yat-Sen, but Jieling's history teachers had bored her to tears). Imperial and countrified.

Then a man came in from human resources.

"There are many kinds of stealing," he began. "There is stealing of money or food. And there is stealing of ideas. Here at New Life, our ideas are like gold, and we guard against having them stolen. But you will learn many secrets, about what we are doing, about how we do things. This is necessary as you do your work. If you tell our secrets, that is theft. And we will find out." He paused here and looked at them in what was clearly intended to be a very frightening way.

Jieling looked down at the ground because it was like watching someone overact. It was embarrassing. Her new shoes were very white and clean.

Then he outlined the prison terms for industrial espionage. Ten, twenty years in prison. "China must take its place as an innovator on the world stage and so must respect the laws of intellectual property," he intoned. It was part of the modernization of China, where technology was a new future—Jieling put on her "I am a good girl" face. It was like politics class. Four modernizations. Six goals. Sometimes when she was a little girl, and she was riding behind her father on his bike to school, he would pass a billboard with a saying about traffic safety and begin to recite quotes from Mao. *The force at the core of the revolution is the people!* He would tuck his chin in when he did this and use a very serious voice, like a movie or like opera. *Western experience for Chinese uses.* Some of them she had learned from him. *All reactionaries are paper tigers!* she would chant with him, trying to make her voice deep. *Be resolute, fear no sacrifice, and surmount every difficulty to win victory!* And then she would start giggling and he would glance over his shoulder and grin at her. He had been a Red Guard when he was young, but other than this, he never talked about it.

After the lecture, they were taken to be paired with workers who would train them. At least she didn't have to go with the Manchu girl, who was led off to shipping.

She was paired with a very small girl in one of the culture rooms. "I am Baiyue," the girl said. Baiyue was so tiny, only up to Jieling's shoulder, that her green scrubs swamped her. She had pigtails. The room where they worked was filled with rows and rows of what looked like wide drawers. Down the center of the room was a long table with petri dishes and trays and lab equipment. Jieling didn't know what some of it was, and that was a little nerve-wracking. All up and down the room, pairs of girls in green worked at either the drawers or the table.

"We're going to start cultures," Baiyue said. "Take a tray and fill it with those." She pointed to a stack of petri dishes. The bottom of each dish was filled with gelatin. Jieling took a tray and did what Baiyue did. Baiyue was serious but not at all sharp or superior. She explained that what they were doing was seeding the petri dishes with cells.

"Cells?" Jieling asked.

"Nerve cells from the electric ray. It's a fish."

They took swabs, and Baiyue showed her how to put the cells on in a zigzag motion so that most of the gel was covered. They did six trays full of petri dishes. They didn't smell fishy. Then they used pipettes to put in feeding solution. It was all pleasantly scientific without being very difficult.

At one point everybody left for lunch, but Baiyue said they couldn't go until they got the cultures finished or the batch would be ruined. Women shuffled by them, and Jieling's stomach growled. But when the lab was empty, Baiyue smiled and said, "Where are you from?"

Baiyue was from Fujian. "If you ruin a batch," she explained, "you have to pay out of your paycheck. I'm almost out of debt, and when I get clear—"she glanced around and dropped her voice a little "—I can quit."

"Why are you in debt?" Jieling asked. Maybe this was harder than she thought; maybe Baiyue had screwed up in the past.

"Everyone is in debt," Baiyue said. "It's just the way they run things. Let's get the trays in the warmers."

The drawers along the walls opened out, and inside, the temperature was kept blood warm. They loaded the trays into the drawers, one back and one front, going down the row until they had the morning's trays all in.

"Okay," Baiyue said, "that's good. We'll check trays this afternoon. I've got a set for transfer to the tissue room, but we'll have time after we eat."

Jieling had never eaten in the employee cafeteria, only in the guest house restaurant, and only the first night, because it was expensive. Since then she had been living on ramen noodles, and she was starved for a good meal. She smelled garlic and pork. First thing on the food line was a pan of steamed pork buns, fluffy white. But Baiyue headed off to a place at the back where there was a huge pot of congee—rice porridge—kept hot. "It's the cheapest thing in the cafeteria," Baiyue explained, "and you can eat all you want." She dished up a big bowl of it—a lot of congee for a girl her size—and added some salt vegetables and boiled peanuts. "It's pretty good, although usually by lunch it's been sitting a little while. It gets a little gluey."

Jieling hesitated. Baiyue had said she was in debt. Maybe she had to eat this stuff. But Jieling wasn't going to have old rice porridge for lunch. "I'm going to get some rice and vegetables," she said.

Baiyue nodded. "Sometimes I get that. It isn't too bad. But stay away from anything with shrimp in it. Soooo expensive."

Jieling got rice and vegetables and a big pork bun. There were two fish dishes and a pork dish with monkeybrain mushrooms, but she decided she could maybe have the pork for dinner. There was no cost written on anything. She gave her *danwei* card to the woman at the end of the line, who swiped it and handed it back.

"How much?" Jieling asked.

The woman shrugged. "It comes out of your food allowance."

Jieling started to argue, but across the cafeteria, Baiyue was waving her arm in the sea of green scrubs to get Jieling's attention. Baiyue called from a table. "Jieling! Over here!

Baiyue's eyes got very big when Jieling sat down. "A pork bun."

"Are they really expensive?" Jieling asked.

Baiyue nodded. "Like gold. And so good."

Jieling looked around at other tables. Other people were eating the pork and steamed buns and everything else.

"Why are you in debt?" Jieling asked.

Baiyue shrugged. "Everyone is in debt," she said. "Just most people have given up. Everything costs here. Your food, your dormitory, your uniforms. They always make sure that you never earn anything."

"They can't do that!" Jieling said.

Baiyue said, "My granddad says it's like the old days, when you weren't allowed to quit your job. He says I should shut up and be happy. That they take good care of me. Iron rice bowl."

"But, but, but," Jieling dredged the word up from some long forgotten class, "that's *feudal!*"

Baiyue nodded. "Well, that's my granddad. He used to make my brother and me kowtow to him and my grandmother at Spring Festival." She frowned and wrinkled her nose. Country customs. Nobody in the city made their children kowtow at New Year's. "But you're lucky," Baiyue said to Jieling. "You'll have your uniform debt and dormitory fees, but you haven't started on food debt or anything."

Jieling felt sick. "I stayed in the guest house for four days," she said. "They said they would charge it against my wages."

"Oh," Baiyue covered her mouth with her hand. After a moment, she said, "Don't worry, we'll figure something out." Jieling felt more frightened by that than anything else.

Instead of going back to the lab they went upstairs and across a connecting bridge to the dormitories. Naps? Did they get naps?

"Do you know what room you're in?" Baiyue asked.

Jieling didn't. Baiyue took her to ask the floor auntie, who looked up Jieling's name and gave her a key and some sheets and a blanket. Back down the hall and around the corner. The room was spare but really nice. Two bunk beds and two chests of drawers, a concrete floor. It had a window. All of the beds were taken except one of the top ones. By the window under the desk were three black boxes hooked to the wall. They were a little bigger than a shoebox. Baiyue flipped open the front of each one. They had names written on them. "Here's a space where we can put your battery." She pointed to an electrical extension.

"What are they?" Jieling said.

"They're the battery boxes. It's what we make. I'll get you one that failed inspection. A lot of them work fine," Baiyue said. "Inside there are electric ray cells to make electricity, and symbiotic bacteria. The bacteria breaks down garbage to feed the ray cells. Garbage turned into electricity. Anti–global warming. No greenhouse gas. You have to feed it scraps from the cafeteria a couple of times a week or it will die, but it does best if you feed it a little bit every day."

"It's alive?!" Jieling said.

Baiyue shrugged. "Yeah. Sort of. Supposedly if it does really well, you get credits for the electricity it generates. They charge us for our electricity use, so this helps hold down debt."

The three boxes just sat there looking less alive than a boom box.

"Can you see the cells?" Jieling asked.

Baiyue shook her head. "No, the feed mechanism doesn't let you. They're just like the ones we grow, though, only they've been worked on in the tissue room. They added bacteria."

"Can it make you sick?"

"No, the bacteria can't live in people." Baiyue said. "Can't live anywhere except in the box."

"And it makes electricity."

Baiyue nodded.

"And people can buy it?"

She nodded again. "We've just started selling them. They say they're going to sell them in China, but really, they're too expensive. Americans like them, you know, because of the no-global-warming. Of course, Americans buy anything."

The boxes were on the wall between the beds, under the window, pretty near where the pillows were on the bottom bunks. She hadn't minded the cells in the lab, but this whole thing was too creepy.

Jieling's first paycheck was startling. She owed 1,974 R.M.B. Almost four month's salary if she never ate or bought anything and if she didn't have a dorm room. She went back to her room and climbed into her bunk and looked at the figures. Money deducted for uniforms and shoes, food, her time in the guesthouse.

Her roommates came chattering in a group. Jieling's roommates all worked in packaging. They were nice enough, but they had been friends before Jieling moved in.

"Hey," called Taohua. Then, seeing what Jieling had. "Oh, first paycheck."

Jieling nodded. It was like getting a jail sentence.

"Let's see. Oh, not so bad. I owe three times that," Taohua said. She passed the statement on to the other girls. All the girls owed huge amounts. More than a year.

"Don't you care?" Jieling said.

"You mean like little Miss Lei Feng?" Taohua asked. Everyone laughed and Jieling laughed, too, although her face heated up. Miss Lei Feng was what they called Baiyue. Little Miss Goody-goody. Lei Feng, the famous do-gooder soldier who darned his friend's socks on the Long March. He was nobody when he was alive, but when he died, his diary listed all the anonymous good deeds he had done, and then he became a Hero. Lei Feng posters hung in elementary schools. He wanted to be "a revolutionary screw that never rusts." It was the kind of thing everybody's grandparents had believed in.

"Does Baiyue have a boyfriend?" Taohua asked, suddenly serious.

"No, no!" Jieling said. It was against the rules to have a boyfriend, and Baiyue was always getting in trouble for breaking rules. Things like not having her trays stacked by 5:00 p.m., although nobody else got in trouble for that.

"If she had a boyfriend," Taohua said, "I could see why she would want to quit. You can't get married if you're in debt. It would be too hard."

"Aren't you worried about your debt?" Jieling asked.

Taohua laughed. "I don't have a boyfriend. And besides, I just got a promotion, so soon I'll pay off my debt."

"You'll have to stop buying clothes," one of the other girls said. The company store did have a nice catalog you could order clothes from, but they were expensive. There was debt limit, based on your salary. If you were promoted, your debt limit would go up.

"Or I'll go to special projects," Taohua said. Everyone knew what special projects was, even though it was supposed to be a big company secret. They were computers made of bacteria. They looked a lot like the boxes in the dormitory rooms. "I've been studying computers," Taohua explained. "Bacterial computers are special. They do many things. They can detect chemicals. They are *massively* parallel."

"What does that mean?" Jieling asked.

"It is hard to explain," Taohua said evasively.

Taohua opened her battery and poured in scraps. It was interesting that Taohua claimed not to care about her debt but kept feeding her battery. Jieling had a battery now, too. It was a reject—the back had broken so that the metal things that sent the electricity back out were exposed, and if you touched it wrong, it could give you a shock. No problem, since Jieling had plugged it into the wall and didn't plan to touch it again.

"Besides," Taohua said, "I like it here a lot better than at home."

Better than home. In some ways, yes, in some ways, no. What would it be like to just give up and belong to the company? Nice things, nice food. Never rich. But never poor, either. Medical care. Maybe it wasn't the worst thing. Maybe Baiyue was a little … obsessive.

"I don't care about my debt," Taohua said serenely. "With one more promotion, I'll move to cadres housing."

Jieling reported the conversation to Baiyue. They were getting incubated cells ready to move to the tissue room. In the tissue room they'd be transferred to the protein and collagen grid that would guide their growth—line up the cells to approximate an electricity-generating system. The tissue room had a weird, yeasty smell.

"She's fooling herself," Baiyue said. "Line girls never get to be cadres. She might get onto special projects, but that's even worse than regular line work, because you're never allowed to leave the compound." Baiyue picked up a dish, stuck a little volt reader into the gel, and rapped the dish smartly against the lab table.

The needle on the volt gauge swung to indicate the cells had discharged electricity. That was the way they tested to see if the cells were generating electricity. A shock made them discharge, and the easiest way was to knock them against the table.

Baiyue could sound very bitter about New Life. Jieling didn't like the debt; it scared her a little. But, really, Baiyue saw only one side of everything. "I thought you got a pay raise to go to special projects," Jieling said.

Baiyue rolled her eyes. "And more reasons to go in debt, I'll bet."

"How much is your debt?" Jieling asked.

"Still seven hundred," Baiyue said. "Because they told me I had to have new uniforms." She sighed.

"I am so sick of congee," Jieling said. "They're never going to let us get out of debt."

Baiyue's way was doomed. She was trying to play by the company's rules and still win. That wasn't Jieling's way. "We have to make money somewhere else," Jieling said.

"Right," Baiyue said. "We work six days a week." And Baiyue often stayed after shift to try to make sure she didn't lose wages on failed cultures. "Out of spec," she'd say and put it aside. She had taught Jieling to keep the out-of-specs for a day. Sometimes they improved and could be shipped on. It wasn't the way the supervisor, Ms. Wang, explained the job to Jieling, but it cut down on the number of rejects, and that, in turn, cut down on paycheck deductions.

"That leaves us Sundays," Jieling said.

"I can't leave compound this Sunday."

"And if you do, what are they going to do, fire you?" Jieling said.

"I don't think we're supposed to earn money outside the compound," Baiyue said.

"You are too much of a good girl," Jieling said. "Remember, *it doesn't matter if the cat is black or white, as long as it catches mice.*"

"Is that Mao?" Baiyue asked, frowning.

"No," Jieling said, "Deng Xiaoping, the one after Mao."

"Well, he's dead, too," Baiyue said. She rapped a dish against the counter, and the needle on the volt meter jumped.

Jieling had been working just over four weeks when they were all called to the cafeteria for a meeting. Mr. Cao from human resources was there. He was wearing a dark suit and standing at the white screen. Other cadres sat in chairs along the back of the stage, looking very stern.

"We are here to discuss a very serious matter," he said. "Many of you know this girl."

There was a laptop hooked up and a very nervous-looking boy running it. Jieling looked carefully at the laptop, but it didn't appear to be a special projects computer. In fact, it was made in Korea. He did something, and an ID picture of a girl flashed on the screen.

Jieling didn't know her. But around her she heard noises of shock, someone sucking air through their teeth. Someone else breathed softly, '*Ai-yah.*'

"This girl ran away, leaving her debt with New Life. She ate our food, wore our clothes, slept in our beds. And then, like a thief, she ran away." The Human Resources man nodded his head. The boy at the computer changed the image on the big projector screen.

Now it was a picture of the same girl with her head bowed and two policemen holding her arms.

"She was picked up in Guangdong," the human resources man said. She is in jail there."

The cafeteria was very quiet.

The human resources man said, "Her life is ruined, which is what should happen to all thieves."

Then he dismissed them. That afternoon, the picture of the girl with the two policemen appeared on the bulletin boards of every floor of the dormitory.

On Sunday, Baiyue announced, "I'm not going."

She was not supposed to leave the compound, but one of her roommates had female problems—bad cramps—and planned to spend the day in bed drinking tea and reading magazines. Baiyue was going to use her ID to leave.

"You have to," Jieling said. "You want to grow old here? Die a serf to New Life?"

"It's crazy. We can't make money dancing in the plague-trash market."

"I've done it before," Jieling said. "You're scared."

"It's just not a good idea," Baiyue said.

"Because of the girl they caught in Guangdong. We're not skipping out on our debt. We're paying it off."

"We're not supposed to work for someone else when we work here," Baiyue said.

"Oh, come on," Jieling said. "You are always making things sound worse than they are. I think you like staying here being little Miss Lei Feng."

"Don't call me that," Baiyue snapped.

"Well, don't act like it. New Life is not being fair. We don't have to be fair. What are they going to do to you if they catch you?"

"Fine me," Baiyue said. "Add to my debt!"

"So what? They're going to find a way to add to your debt no matter what. You are a serf. They are the landlord."

"But if—"

"No *but if.*" Jieling said. "You like being a martyr. I don't."

"What do you care," Baiyue said. "You like it here. If you stay you can eat pork buns every night."

"And you can eat congee for the rest of your life. I'm going to try to do something." Jieling slammed out of the dorm room. She had never said harsh things to Baiyue before. Yes, she had thought about staying here. But was that so bad? Better than being like Baiyue, who would stay here and have a miserable life. Jieling was not going to have a miserable life, no matter where she stayed or what she did. That was why she had come to Shenzhen in the first place.

She heard the door open behind her, and Baiyue ran down the hall. "Okay," she said breathlessly. "I'll try it. Just this once."

The streets of Shanghai were incredibly loud after weeks in the compound. In a shop window, she and Baiyue stopped and watched a news segment on how the fashion in Shanghai was for sarongs. Jieling would have to tell her mother. Of course, her mother had a TV and probably already knew. Jieling thought about calling, but not now. Not now. She didn't want to explain about New Life. The next news segment was about the success of the People's Army in Tajikistan. Jieling pulled Baiyue to come on.

They took one bus and then had to transfer. On Sundays, unless you were lucky, it took forever to transfer because fewer buses ran. They waited almost an hour for the second bus. That bus was almost empty when they got on. They sat down a few seats back from the driver. Baiyue rolled her eyes. "Did you see the guy in the back?" she asked. "Party functionary."

Jieling glanced over her shoulder and saw him. She couldn't miss him, in his careful polo shirt. He had that stiff party-member look.

Baiyue sighed. "My uncle is just like that. So *boring.*"

Jieling thought that, to be honest, Baiyue would have made a good revolutionary, back in the day. Baiyue liked that kind of revolutionary purity. But she nodded.

The plague-trash market was full on a Sunday. There was a toy seller making tiny little clay figures on sticks. He waved a stick at the girls as they passed. "Cute things!" he called. "I'll make whatever you want!" The stick had a little Donald Duck on it.

"I can't do this," Baiyue said. "There's too many people."

"It's not so bad," Jieling said. She found a place for the boom box. Jieling had brought them to where all the food vendors were. "Stay here and watch this," she said. She hunted through the food stalls and bought a bottle of local beer, counting out from the little horde of money she had left from when she had come. She took the beer back to Baiyue. "Drink this," she said. "It will help you be brave."

"I hate beer," Baiyue said.

"Beer or debt," Jieling said.

47

While Baiyue drank the beer, Jieling started the boom box and did her routine. People smiled at her, but no one put any money in her cash box. Shenzhen people were so cheap. Baiyue sat on the curb, nursing her beer, not looking at Jieling or at anyone until finally Jieling couldn't stand it any longer.

"C'mon *meimei,*" she said.

Baiyue seemed a bit surprised to be called little sister, but she put the beer down and got up. They had practiced a routine to an M.I.A. song, singing and dancing. It would be a hit, Jieling was sure.

"I can't," Baiyue whispered.

"Yes you can," Jieling said. "You do good."

A couple of people stopped to watch them arguing, so Jieling started the music.

"I feel sick," Baiyue whimpered.

But the beat started, and there was nothing to do but dance and sing. Baiyue was so nervous, she forgot at first, but then she got the hang of it. She kept her head down, and her face was bright red.

Jieling started making up a rap. She'd never done it before, and she hadn't gotten very far before she was laughing and then Baiyue was laughing, too.

Wode meimei hen haixiude
Mei ta shi xuli
tai hen xiuqi—

My little sister is so shy
But she's pretty
Far too delicate—

They almost stopped because they were giggling, but they kept dancing, and Jieling went back to the lyrics from the song they had practiced.

When they had finished, people clapped, and they'd made thirty-two yuan.

They didn't make as much for any single song after that, but in a few hours they had collected 187 yuan. It was early evening, and night entertainers were showing up—a couple of people who sang opera, acrobats, and a clown with a wig of hair so red it looked on fire, stepping stork-legged on stilts waving a rubber Kalashnikov in his hand. He was all dressed in white. Uncle Death, from cartoons during the plague. Some of the day vendors had shut down, and new people were showing up who put out a board and some chairs and served sorghum liquor; clear, white, and 150 proof. The crowd was starting to change, too. It was rowdier. Packs of young men dressed in weird combinations of clothes from plague markets—vintage Mao suit jackets and suit pants and peasant shoes. And others, veterans from the Tajikistan conflict, one with an empty trouser leg.

Jieling picked up the boom box, and Baiyue took the cash box. Outside of the market, it wasn't yet dark.

"You are amazing," Baiyue kept saying. "You are such a special girl!"

"You did great," Jieling said. "When I was by myself, I didn't make anything! Everyone likes you because you are little and cute!"

"Look at this! I'll be out of debt before autumn!"

Maybe it was just the feeling that she was responsible for Baiyue, but Jieling said, "You keep it all."

"I can't! I can't! We split it!" Baiyue said.

"Sure," Jieling said. "Then after you get away, you can help me. Just think, if we do this for three more Sundays, you'll pay off your debt."

"Oh, Jieling," Baiyue said. "You really are like my big sister!"

Jieling was sorry she had ever called Baiyue "little sister." It was such a country thing to do. She had always suspected that Baiyue wasn't a city girl. Jieling hated the countryside. Grain spread to dry in the road and mother's-elder-sister and father's-younger-brother bringing all the cousins over on the day off. Jieling didn't even know all those country ways to say aunt and uncle. It wasn't Baiyue's fault. And Baiyue had been good to her. She was rotten to be thinking this way.

"Excuse me," said a man. He wasn't like the packs of young men with their long hair and plague clothes. Jieling couldn't place him, but he seemed familiar. "I saw you in the market. You were very fun. Very lively."

Baiyue took hold of Jieling's arm. For a moment Jieling wondered if maybe he was from New Life, but she told herself that that was crazy. "Thank you," she said. She thought she remembered him putting ten yuan in the box. No, she thought, he was on the bus. The party functionary. The party was checking up on them. Now *that* was funny. She wondered if he would lecture them on Western ways.

"Are you in the music business?" Baiyue asked. She glanced at Jieling, who couldn't help laughing, snorting through her nose.

The man took them very seriously, though. "No," he said. "I can't help you there. But I like your act. You seem like girls of good character."

"Thank you," Baiyue said. She didn't look at Jieling again, which was good, because Jieling knew she wouldn't be able to keep a straight face.

"I am Wei Rongyi. Maybe I can buy you some dinner?" the man asked. He held up his hands, "Nothing romantic. You are so young, it is like you could be daughters."

"You have a daughter?" Jieling asked.

He shook his head. "Not anymore," he said.

Jieling understood. His daughter had died of the bird flu. She felt embarrassed for having laughed at him. Her soft heart saw instantly that he was treating them like the daughter he had lost.

He took them to a dumpling place on the edge of the market and ordered half a kilo of crescent-shaped pork dumplings and a kilo of square beef dumplings. He was a cadre, a middle manager. His wife had lived in Changsha for a couple of years now, where her family was from. He was from the older generation, people who did not get divorced. All around them, the restaurant was filling up mostly with men stopping after work for dumplings and drinks. They were a little island surrounded by truck drivers and men who worked in the factories in the outer city—tough, grimy places.

"What do you do? Are you secretaries?" Wei Rongyi asked.

Baiyue laughed. "As if!" she said.

"We are factory girls," Jieling said. She dunked a dumpling in vinegar. They were so good! Not congee!

"Factory girls!" he said. "I am so surprised!"

Baiyue nodded. "We work for New Life," she explained. "This is our day off, so we wanted to earn a little extra money."

He rubbed his head, looking off into the distance. "New Life," he said, trying to place the name. "New Life ..."

"Out past the zoo," Baiyue said.

Jieling thought they shouldn't say so much.

"Ah, in the city. A good place? What do they make?" he asked. He had a way of blinking very quickly that was disconcerting.

"Batteries," Jieling said. She didn't say bio-batteries.

"I thought they made computers," he said.

"Oh, yes," Baiyue said. "Special projects."

Jieling glared at Baiyue. If this guy gave them trouble at New Life, they'd have a huge problem getting out of the compound.

Baiyue blushed.

Wei laughed. "You are special project girls, then. Well, see, I knew you were not just average factory girls."

He didn't press the issue. Jieling kept waiting for him to make some sort of move on them. Offer to buy them beer. But he didn't, and when they had finished their dumplings, he gave them the leftovers to take back to their dormitories and then stood at the bus stop until they were safely on their bus.

"Are you sure you will be all right?" he asked them when the bus came.

"You can see my window from the bus stop," Jieling promised. "We will be fine."

"Shenzhen can be a dangerous city. You be careful!"

Out the window, they could see him in the glow of the street-light, waving as the bus pulled away.

"He was so nice," Baiyue sighed. "Poor man."

"Didn't you think he was a little strange?" Jieling asked.

"Everybody is strange nowadays," Baiyue said. "After the plague. Not like when we were growing up."

It was true. Her mother was strange. Lots of people were crazy from so many people dying.

Jieling held up the leftover dumplings. "Well, anyway. I am not feeding this to my battery," she said. They both tried to smile.

"Our whole generation is crazy," Baiyue said.

"We know everybody dies," Jieling said. Outside the bus window, the streets were full of young people, out trying to live while they could.

They made all their bus connections as smooth as silk. So quick, they were home in forty-five minutes. Sunday night was movie night, and all of Jieling's roommates were at the movie, so she and Baiyue could sort the money in Jieling's room. She used her key card, and the door clicked open.

Mr. Wei was kneeling by the battery boxes in their room. He started and hissed, "Close the door!"

Jieling was so surprised, she did.

"Mr. Wei!" Baiyue said.

He was dressed like an army man on a secret mission, all in black. He showed them a little black gun. Jieling blinked in surprise. "Mr. Wei!" she said. It was hard to take him seriously. Even all in black, he was still weird Mr. Wei, blinking rapidly behind his glasses.

"Lock the door," he said. "And be quiet."

"The door locks by itself," Jieling explained. "And my room-mates will be back soon."

"Put a chair in front of the door," he said and shoved the desk chair toward them. Baiyue pushed it under the door handle. The window was open, and Jieling could see where he had climbed on the desk and left a footprint on Taohua's fashion magazine. Taohua was going to be pissed. And what was Jieling going to say? If anyone found out there had been a man in her room, she was going to be in very big trouble.

"How did you get in?" she asked. "What about the cameras?" There were security cameras.

He showed them a little spray can. "Special paint. It just makes things look foggy and dim. Security guards are so lazy now, no one ever checks things out." He paused a moment, clearly disgusted with the lax morality of the day. "Miss Jieling," he said. "Take that screw-driver and finish unscrewing that computer from the wall."

Computer? She realized he meant the battery boxes.

Baiyue's eyes got very big. "Mr. Wei! You're a thief!"

Jieling shook her head. "A corporate spy."

"I am a patriot," he said. "But you young people wouldn't under-stand that. Sit on the bed." He waved the gun at Baiyue.

The gun was so little it looked like a toy, and it was difficult to be afraid, but still Jieling thought it was good that Baiyue sat.

Jieling knelt. It was her box that Mr. Wei had been disconnect-ing. It was all the way to the right, so he had started with it. She had come to feel a little bit attached to it, thinking of it sitting there, occa-sionally zapping electricity back into the grid, reducing her electricity costs and her debt. She sighed and unscrewed it. Mr. Wei watched.

She jimmied it off the wall, careful not to touch the contacts. The cells built up a charge, and when they were ready, a switch tapped a membrane and they discharged. It was all automatic, and there was no knowing when it was going to happen. Mr. Wei was going to be very upset when he realized that this wasn't a computer.

"Put it on the desk," he said.

She did.

"Now sit with your friend."

Jieling sat down next to Baiyue. Keeping a wary eye on them, he sidled over to the bio-battery. He opened the hatch where they dumped garbage in them, and he tried to look in as well as look at them. "Where are the controls?" he asked. He picked it up, his palm flat against the broken back end where the contacts were exposed.

"Tap it against the desk," Jieling said. "Sometimes the door sticks." There wasn't actually a door. But it had just come into her head. She hoped that the cells hadn't discharged in a while.

Mr. Wei frowned and tapped the box smartly against the desktop.

Torpedinidae, the electric ray, can generate a current of two hundred volts for approximately a minute. The power output is close to one kilowatt over the course of the discharge, and while this won't kill the average person, it is a powerful shock. Mr. Wei stiffened and fell, clutching the box and spasming wildly. One ... two ... three ... four ... Mr. Wei was still spasming. Jieling and Baiyue looked at each other. Gingerly, Jieling stepped around Mr. Wei. He had dropped the little gun. Jieling picked it up. Mr. Wei was still spasming. Jieling wondered if he was going to die. Or if he was already dead and the electricity was just making him jump. She didn't want him to die. She looked at the little gun, and it made her feel even sicker, so she threw it out the window.

Finally, Mr. Wei dropped the box.

Baiyue said, "Is he dead?"

Jieling was afraid to touch him. She couldn't tell if he was breathing. Then he groaned, and both girls jumped.

"He's not dead," Jieling said.

"What should we do?" Baiyue asked.

"Tie him up," Jieling said. Although she wasn't sure what they'd do with him then.

Jieling used the cord to her boom box to tie his wrists. When she grabbed his hands, he gasped and struggled feebly. Then she took her pillowcase and cut along the blind end, a space just wide enough that his head would fit through.

"Sit him up," she said to Baiyue.

"You sit him up," Baiyue said. Baiyue didn't want to touch him.

Jieling pulled Mr. Wei into a sitting position. "Put the pillowcase over his head," she said. The pillowcase was like a shirt with no arm-holes, so when Baiyue pulled it over his head and shoulders, it pinned his arms against his sides and worked something like a straitjacket.

Jieling took his wallet and identification papers out of his pocket. "Why would someone carry their wallet to a break in?" she asked. "He has six ID papers. One says he is Mr. Wei."

"Wow," Baiyue said. "Let me see. Also Mr. Ma. Mr. Zhang. Two Mr. Liu's and a Mr. Cui."

Mr. Wei blinked, his eyes watering.

"Do you think he has a weak heart?" Baiyue asked.

"I don't know," Jieling said. "Wouldn't he be dead if he did?"

Baiyue considered this.

"Baiyue! Look at all this yuan!" Jieling emptied the wallet, count-ing. Almost eight thousand yuan!

"Let me go," Mr. Wei said weakly.

Jieling was glad he was talking. She was glad he seemed like he might be all right. She didn't know what they would do if he died. They would never be able to explain a dead person. They would end up in deep debt. And probably go to jail for something. "Should we call the floor auntie and tell her that he broke in?" Jieling asked.

"We could," Baiyue said.

"Do not!" Mr. Wei said, sounding stronger. "You don't under-stand! I'm from Beijing!"

"So is my stepfather," Jieling said. "Me, I'm from Baoding. It's about an hour south of Beijing."

Mr. Wei said, "I'm from the government! That money is government money!"

"I don't believe you," Jieling said. "Why did you come in through the window?" Jieling asked.

"Secret agents always come in through the window?" Baiyue said and started to giggle.

"Because this place is counterrevolutionary!" Mr. Wei said.

Baiyue covered her mouth with her hand. Jieling felt embarrassed, too. No one said things like "counterrevolutionary" anymore.

"This place! It is making things that could make China strong!" he said.

"Isn't that good?" Baiyue asked.

"But they don't care about China! Only about money. Instead of using it for China, they sell it to America!" he said. Spittle was gathering at the corner of his mouth. He was starting to look deranged. "Look at this place! Officials are all concerned about *guanxi*!" Connections. Kickbacks. *Guanxi* ran China, everybody knew that.

"So, maybe you have an anticorruption investigation?" Jieling said. There were lots of anticorruption investigations. Jieling's stepfather said that they usually meant someone powerful was mad at their brother-in-law or something, so they accused them of corruption.

Mr. Wei groaned. "There is no one to investigate them."

Baiyue and Jieling looked at each other.

Mr. Wei explained, "In my office, the Guangdong office, there used to be twenty people. Special operatives. Now there is only me and Ms. Yang."

Jieling said, "Did they all die of bird flu?"

Mr. Wei shook his head. "No, they all went to work on contract for Saudi Arabia. You can make a lot of money in the Middle East. A lot more than in China."

"Why don't you and Ms. Yang go work in Saudi Arabia?" Baiyue asked.

Jieling thought Mr. Wei would give some revolutionary speech. But he just hung his head. "She is the secretary. I am the bookkeeper." And then, in a smaller voice, "She is going to Kuwait to work for Mr. Liu."

They probably did not need bookkeepers in the Middle East. Poor Mr. Wei. No wonder he was such a terrible secret agent.

"The spirit of the revolution is gone," he said, and there were real, honest-to-goodness tears in his eyes. "Did you know that Tiananmen Square was built by volunteers? People would come after their regular jobs and lay the paving of the square. Today people look to Hong Kong."

"Nobody cares about a bunch of old men in Beijing," Baiyue said.

"Exactly! We used to have a strong military! But now the military is too worried about their own factories and farms! They want us to pull out of Tajikistan because it is ruining their profits!"

This sounded like a good idea to Jieling, but she had to admit, she hated the news, so she wasn't sure why they were fighting in Tajikistan anyway. Something about Muslim terrorists. All she knew about Muslims was that they made great street food.

"Don't you want to be patriots?" Mr. Wei said.

"You broke into my room and tried to steal my—you know that's not a computer, don't you?" Jieling said. "It's a bio-battery. They're selling them to the Americans. Wal-Mart."

Mr. Wei groaned.

"We don't work in special projects," Baiyue said.

"You said you did," he protested.

"We did not," Jieling said. "You just thought that. How did you know this was my room?"

"The company lists all its workers in a directory," he said wearily. "And it's movie night, everyone is either out or goes to the movies. I've had the building under surveillance for weeks. I followed you to the market today. Last week it was a girl named Pingli, who blabbed about everything, but she wasn't in special projects.

"I put you on the bus; I've timed the route three times. I should have had an hour and fifteen minutes to drive over here and get the box and get out."

"We made all our connections," Baiyue explained.

Mr. Wei was so dispirited he didn't even respond.

Jieling said. "I thought the government was supposed to help workers. If we get caught, we'll be fined, and we'll be deeper in debt." She was just talking. Talking, talking, talking too much. This was too strange. Like when someone was dying. Something extraordinary was happening, like your father dying in the next room, and yet the ordinary things went on, too. You made tea, your mother opened the shop the next day and sewed clothes while she cried. People came in and pretended not to notice. This was like that. Mr. Wei had a gun, and they were explaining about New Life.

"Debt?" Mr. Wei said.

"To the company," she said. "We are all in debt. The company hires us and says they are going to pay us, but then they charge us for our food and our clothes and our dorm, and it always costs more than we earn. That's why we were doing rap today. To make money to be able to quit." Mr. Wei's glasses had tape holding the arm on. Why hadn't she noticed that in the restaurant? Maybe because when you are afraid, you notice things. When your father is dying of the plague, you notice the way the covers on your mother's chairs need to be washed. You wonder if you will have to do it, or if you will die before you have to do chores.

"The Pingli girl," he said, "she said the same thing. That's illegal."

"Sure," Baiyue said. "Like anybody cares."

"Could you expose corruption?" Jieling asked.

Mr. Wei shrugged, at least as much as he could in the pillowcase. "Maybe. But they would just pay bribes to locals, and it would all go away."

All three of them sighed.

"Except," Mr. Wei said, sitting up a little straighter. "The Americans. They are always getting upset about that sort of thing. Last year there was a corporation, the Shanghai Six. The Americans did a documentary on them, and then Western companies would not do business. If they got information from us about what New Life is doing ..."

"Who else is going to buy bio-batteries?" Baiyue said. "The company would be in big trouble!"

"Beijing can threaten a big exposé, tell the *New York Times* newspaper!" Mr. Wei said, getting excited. "My Beijing supervisor will love that! He loves media!"

"Then you can have a big show trial," Jieling said.

Mr. Wei was nodding.

"But what is in it for us?" Baiyue said.

"When there's a trial, they'll have to cancel your debt!" Mr. Wei said. "Even pay you a big fine!"

"If I call the floor auntie and say I caught a corporate spy, they'll give me a big bonus," Baiyue said.

"Don't you care about the other workers?" Mr. Wei asked.

Jieling and Baiyue looked at each other and shrugged. Did they? "What are they going to do to you, anyway?" Jieling said. "You can still do big exposé. But that way we don't have to wait."

"Look," he said, "you let me go, and I'll let you keep my money." Someone rattled the door handle.

"Please," Mr. Wei whispered. "You can be heroes for your fellow workers, even though they'll never know it."

Jieling stuck the money in her pocket. Then she took the papers, too.

"You can't take those," he said.

"Yes I can," she said. "If after six months, there is no big corruption scandal? We can let everyone know how a government secret agent was outsmarted by two factory girls."

"Six months!" he said. "That's not long enough!"

"It better be," Jieling said.

Outside the door, Taohua called, "Jieling? Are you in there? Something is wrong with the door!"

"Just a minute," Jieling called. "I had trouble with it when I came home." To Mr. Wei she whispered sternly, "Don't you try anything. If you do, we'll scream our heads off, and everybody will come running." She and Baiyue shimmied the pillowcase off of Mr. Wei's head. He started to stand up and jerked the boom box, which clattered across the floor. "Wait!" she hissed and untied him.

Taohua called through the door, "What's that?"

"Hold on!" Jieling called.

Baiyue helped Mr. Wei stand up. Mr. Wei climbed onto the desk and then grabbed a line hanging outside. He stopped a moment as if trying to think of something to say.

"'A revolution is not a dinner party, or writing an essay, or painting a picture, or doing embroidery,'" Jieling said. It had been her father's favorite quote from Chairman Mao. "'... it cannot be so refined, so leisurely and gentle, so temperate, kind, courteous, restrained and magnanimous. A revolution is an insurrection, an act by which one class overthrows another.'"

Mr. Wei looked as if he might cry, and not because he was moved by patriotism. He stepped back and disappeared. Jieling and Baiyue looked out the window. He did go down the wall just like a secret agent from a movie, but it was only two stories. There was still the big footprint in the middle of Taohua's magazine, and the room looked as if it had been hit by a storm.

"They're going to think you had a boyfriend," Baiyue whispered to Jieling.

"Yeah," Jieling said, pulling the chair out from under the door handle. "And they're going to think he's rich."

———

It was Sunday, and Jieling and Baiyue were sitting on the beach. Jieling's cell phone rang, a little chime of M.I.A. hip-hop. Even though it was Sunday, it was one of the girls from New Life. Sunday should be a day off, but she took the call anyway.

"Jieling? This is Xia Meili? From packaging. Taohua told me about your business? Maybe you could help me?"

Jieling said, "Sure. What is your debt, Meili?"

"3,800 R.M.B.," Meili said. "I know it's a lot."

Jieling said, "Not so bad. We have a lot of people who already have loans, though, and it will probably be a few weeks before I can make you a loan."

With Mr. Wei's capital, Jieling and Baiyue had opened a bank account. They had bought themselves out, and then started a little loan business where they bought people out of New Life. Then people had to pay them back with a little extra. They had each had jobs—Jieling worked for a company that made toys. She sat each day at a table where she put a piece of specially shaped plastic over the body of a little doll, an action figure. The plastic fit right over the figure and had cut-outs. Jieling sprayed the whole thing with red paint, and when the piece of plastic was lifted, the action figure had a red shirt. It was boring, but at the end of the week, she got paid instead of owing the company money.

She and Baiyue used all their extra money on loans to get girls out of New Life. More and more loans, and more and more payments. Now New Life had sent them a threatening letter saying that what they were doing was illegal. But Mr. Wei said not to worry. Two officials had come and talked to them and had showed them legal documents and had them explain everything about what had happened. Soon, the officials promised, they would take New Life to court.

Jieling wasn't so sure about the officials. After all, Mr. Wei was an official. But a foreign newspaperman had called them. He was from a newspaper called the *Wall Street Journal*, and he said that he was writing a story about labor shortages in China after the bird flu. He said that in some places in the West there were reports of slavery. His Chinese was very good. His story was going to come out in the United States tomorrow. Then she figured officials would have to do something or lose face.

Jieling told Meili to call her back in two weeks—although hopefully in two weeks no one would need help to get away from New Life—and wrote a note to herself in her little notebook.

Baiyue was sitting looking at the water. "This is the first time I've been to the beach," she said.

"The ocean is so big, isn't it."

Baiyue nodded, scuffing at the white sand. "People always say that, but you don't know until you see it."

Jieling said, "Yeah." Funny, she had lived here for months. Baiyue had lived here more than a year. And they had never come to the beach. The beach was beautiful.

"I feel sorry for Mr. Wei," Baiyue said.

"You do?" Jieling said. "Do you think he really had a daughter who died?"

"Maybe," Baiyue said. "A lot of people died."

"My father died," Jieling said.

Baiyue looked at her, a quick little sideways look, then back out at the ocean. "My mother died," she said.

Jieling was surprised. She had never known that Baiyue's mother was dead. They had talked about so much, but never about that. She put her arm around Baiyue's waist, and they sat for a while.

"I feel bad in a way," Baiyue said.

"How come?" Jieling said.

"Because we had to steal capital to fight New Life. That makes us capitalists."

Jieling shrugged.

"I wish it was like when they fought the revolution," Baiyue said. "Things were a lot more simple."

"Yeah," Jieling said, "and they were poor and a lot of them died."

"I know," Baiyue sighed.

Jieling knew what she meant. It would be nice to ... to be sure what was right and what was wrong. Although not if it made you like Mr. Wei.

Poor Mr. Wei. Had his daughter really died?

"Hey," Jieling said, "I've got to make a call. Wait right here." She walked a little down the beach. It was windy and she turned her back to protect the cell phone, like someone lighting a match. "Hello," she said, "hello, Mama, it's me. Jieling."

Useless Things

S eñora?" The man standing at my screen door is travel stained. Migrant, up from Mexico. The dogs haven't heard him come up, but now they erupt in a frenzy of barking to make up for their oversight. I am sitting at the kitchen table, painting a doll, waiting for the timer to tell me to get doll parts curing in the oven in the workshed.

"Hudson, Abby!" I shout, but they don't pay any attention.

The man steps back. "Do you have work? I can, the weeds," he gestures. He is short-legged, long from waist to shoulder. He's probably headed for the Great Lakes area, the place in the U.S. with the best supply of fresh water and the most need of farm labor.

Behind him is my back plot, with the garden running up to the privacy fence. The sky is just starting to pink up with dawn. At this time of year I do a lot of my work before dawn and late in the evening, when it's not hot. That's probably when he has been traveling, too.

I show him the cistern and set him to weeding. I show him where he can plug in his phone to recharge it. I have internet radio on; Elvis Presley died forty-five years ago today, and they're playing "(You're So Square) Baby I Don't Care." I go inside and get him some bean soup.

Hobos used to mark code to tell other hobos where to stop and where to keep going. Teeth to signify a mean dog. A triangle with hands meant that the homeowner had a gun and might use it. A cat meant a nice lady. Today the men use websites and bulletin boards that they follow, when they can, with cheap smartphones. Somewhere I'm on a site as a 'nice lady' or whatever they say today. The railroad runs east of here, and it's sometimes a last spot where trains slow down before they get to the big yard in Belen. Men come up the Rio Grande hoping to hop the train.

I don't like it. I was happy to give someone a meal when I felt anonymous. Handing a bowl of soup to someone who may not have eaten for a few days was an easy way to feel good about myself. That didn't mean I wanted to open a migrant restaurant. I live by myself. Being an economic refugee doesn't make people kind and good, and I feel as if having my place on some website makes me vulnerable. The dogs may bark like fools, but Hudson is some cross between border collie and golden retriever, and Abby is mostly black lab. They are sweet mutts, not good protection dogs, and it doesn't take a genius to figure that out.

I wake at night sometimes now, thinking someone is in my house. Abby sleeps on the other side of the bed, and Hudson sleeps on the floor. Where I live it is brutally dark at night, unless there's a moon— no one wastes power on lights at night. My house is small, two bedrooms, a kitchen, and a family room. I lean over and shake Hudson on the floor, wake him up. "Who's here?" I whisper. Abby sits up, but neither of them hears anything. They pad down the hall with me into the dark front room, and I peer through the window into the shadowy back lot. I wait for them to bark.

Many a night, I don't go back to sleep.

But the man at my door this morning weeds my garden and accepts my bowl of soup and some flour tortillas. He thanks me gravely. He picks up his phone, charging off my system, and shows me a photo of a woman and a child. "My wife and baby," he says. I nod. I don't particularly want to know about his wife and baby, but I can't be rude.

I finish assembling the doll I am working on. I've painted her, assembled all the parts, and hand-rooted all her hair. She is rather cuter than I like. Customers can mix and match parts off of my website—this face with the eye color of their choice, hands curled one way or another. A mix-and-match doll costs about what the migrant will make in two weeks. A few customers want custom dolls and send images to match. Add a zero to the cost.

I am dressing the doll when Abby leaps up, happily roo-rooing. I start, standing, and drop the doll dangling in my hand by one unshod foot.

It hits the floor head first with a thump, and the man gasps in horror.

"It's a doll," I say.

I don't know if he understands, but he realizes. He covers his mouth with his hand and laughs, nervous.

I scoop the doll off the floor. I make reborns. Dolls that look like newborn infants. The point is to make them look almost, but not quite, real. People prefer them a little cuter, a little more perfect than the real thing. I like them best when there is something a little strange, a little off about them. I like them as ugly as most actual newborns, with some aspect that suggests ontology recapitulating phylogeny; that a developing fetus starts as a single-celled organism, and then develops to look like a tiny fish, before passing in stages into its final animal shape. The old theory of ontology recapitulating phylogeny, that the development of the human embryo follows the evolutionary path, is false, of course. But I prefer that my babies remind us that we are really animals. That they be ancient and a little grotesque. Tiny changelings in our house.

I am equally pleased to think of Thanksgiving turkeys as a kind of dinosaur gracing a holiday table. It is probably why I live alone.

"*Que bonita*," he says. How beautiful.

"*Gracias,*" I say. He has brought me the empty bowl. I take it and send him on his way.

I check my email and I have an order for a special. A reborn made to order. It's from a couple in Chicago, Rachel and Ellam Mazar—I have always assumed that it is Rachel who emails me, but the emails never actually identify who is typing. There is a photo attached of an infant. This wouldn't be strange except this is the third request in three years I have had for exactly the same doll.

The dolls are expensive, especially the specials. I went to art school and then worked as a sculptor for a toy company for a few years. I didn't make dolls, I made action figures, especially alien figures and spaceships from the *Kinetics* movies. A whole generation of boys grew up imprinting on toys I had sculpted. When the craze for *Kinetics* passed, the company laid off lots of people, including me. The whole economy was coming apart at the seams. I had been lucky to have a job for as long as I did. I moved to New Mexico because I loved it and it was cheap, and I tried to do sculpting freelance. I worked at a big-box store. Like so many people, my life went into free fall. I bought this place—a little ranch house that had gone into foreclosure, in a place where no one was buying anything and boarded up houses fall in on themselves like mouths without teeth. It was the last of my savings. I started making dolls as a stopgap.

I get by. Between the garden and the little bit of money from the dolls, I can eat. Which is more than some people.

A special will give me money for property tax. My cistern is getting low, and there is no rain coming until the monsoon in June, which is a long way from now. If it's like last year, we won't get enough rain to fill the cistern anyway. I could pay for the water truck to make a delivery, but I don't like this. When I put the specials on my website, I thought about it as a way to make money. I had seen it on another doll site. I am a trained sculptor. I didn't think about why people would ask for specials.

Some people ask me to make infant dolls of their own children. If my mother had bought an infant version of me, I'd have found it pretty disturbing.

One woman bought a special modeled on herself. She wrote me long e-mails about how her mother had been a narcissist, a monster, and how she was going to symbolically mother herself. Her husband was mayor of a city in California, which was how she could afford to have a replica of her infant self. Her emails made me uncomfortable, which I resented. So eventually I passed her on to another doll maker who made toddlers. I figured she could nurture herself up through all the stages of childhood.

Her reborn was very cute. More attractive than she was in the image she sent. She never commented. I don't know that she ever realized.

I suspect the Mazars fall into another category. I have gotten three requests from people who have lost an infant. I tell myself that there is possibly something healing in recreating your dead child as a doll. Each time I have gotten one of these requests, I have very seriously considered taking the specials off my website.

Property tax payments. Water in the cistern.

If the Mazars lost a child—and I don't know that they did, but I have a feeling that I can't shake—it was bad enough that they want a replica. Then a year ago, I got a request for the second.

I thought that maybe Rachel—if it is Rachel who emails me, not Ellam—had meant to send a different image. I sent back an email asking if they were sure that she had sent the right image.

The response was terse. They were sure.

I sent them an email saying if something had happened, I could do repairs.

The response was equally terse. They wanted me to make one.

I searched for them online but could find out nothing about the Mazars of Chicago. They didn't have a presence online. Who had money but no presence online? Were they organized crime? Just very very private? Now, a third doll.

I don't answer the email. Not yet.

Instead I take my laptop out to the shed. Inside the shed is my oven for baking the doll parts between coats of paint. I plug in the computer to recharge and park it on a shelf above eye level. I have my parts cast by Tony in Ohio, an old connection from my days in the toy industry. He makes my copper molds and rotocasts the parts. Usually, though, the specials are a one-off and he sends me the copper super-master of the head so he doesn't have to store it. I rummage through my molds and find the head from the last time I made this doll. I set it on the shelf and look at it.

I rough-sculpt the doll parts in clay, then do a plaster cast of the clay mold. Then from that I make a wax model, looking like some Victorian memorial of an infant that died of jaundice. I have my own recipe for the wax—commercial wax and paraffin and talc. I could tint it pink; most people do. I just like the way they look.

I do the fine sculpting and polishing on the wax model. I carefully pack and ship the model to Tony, and he casts the copper mold. The process is nasty and toxic, not something I can do myself. For the regular dolls, he does a short run of a hundred or so parts in PVC, vinyl, and ships them to me. He keeps those molds in case I need more. For the head of a special, he sends me back a single cast head and the mold.

All of the detail is on the inside of the mold; outside is only the rough outline of the shape. Infants' heads are long from forehead to the back of the skull. Their faces are tiny and low, their jaws like pork-chop bones. They are marvelous and strange mechanisms.

At about seven, I hear Sherie's truck. The dogs erupt.

Sherie and Ed live about a mile and a half up the road. They have a little dairy goat operation. Sherie is six months pregnant and goes into Albuquerque to see an obstetrician. Her dad works at Sandia Labs and makes decent money, so her parents are paying for her medical care. It's a long drive in and back, the truck is old, and Ed doesn't like her to go alone. I ride along, and we pick up supplies. Her mom makes us lunch.

"Goddamn, it's hot," Sherie says as I climb into the little yellow Toyota truck. "How's your water?"

"Getting low," I say. Sherie and Ed have a well.

"I'm worried we might go dry this year," Sherie says. "They keep whining about the aquifer. If we have to buy water, I don't know what we'll do."

Sherie is physically Chinese, one of the thousands of girls adopted out of China in the nineties and at the turn of the century. She said she went through a phase of trying to learn all things Chinese, but she complains that as far as she can tell, the only thing Chinese about her is that she's lactose intolerant.

"I had a migrant at my door this morning," I say.

"Did you feed him?" she asks. She leans into the shift, trying to find the gear, urging the truck into first.

"He weeded my garden," I say.

"They're not going to stop as long as you feed them."

"Like stray cats," I say.

Albuquerque has never been a pretty town. When I came, it was mostly strip malls and big-box stores and suburbs. Ten years of averages of four inches of rain or less have hurt it badly, especially with the loss of the San Juan/Chama water rights. Water is expensive in Albuquerque. Too expensive for Intel, which pulled out. Intel was just a larger blow in a series of blows.

The suburbs are full of walkaway houses—places where homeowners couldn't meet the mortgage payments and just left, the lots now full of trash and windows gone. People who could went north for water. People who couldn't did what people always do when an economy goes soft and rotten: they slid, to rented houses, rented apartments, living in their cars, living with their families, living on the street.

But inside Sherie's parents' home it's still twenty years ago. The countertops are granite. The big-screen plasma TV gets hundreds of channels. The freezer is full of meat and frozen Lean Cuisine. The air conditioner keeps the temperature at a heavenly seventy-five degrees. Sherie's mother, Brenda, is slim, with beautifully styled graying hair. She's a psychologist with a small practice.

Brenda has one of my dolls, which she bought because she likes me. It's always out when I come, but it doesn't fit Brenda's tailored, airily comfortable style. I have never heard Brenda say a thing against Ed. But I can only assume that she and Kyle wish Sherie had married someone who worked at Los Alamos or at Sandia or the university, someone with government benefits like health insurance. On the other hand, Sherie was a wild child who, as Brenda said, "did a stint as a lesbian," as if being a lesbian were like signing up for the Peace Corps. You can't make your child fall in love with the right kind of person. I wish I could have fallen in love with someone from Los Alamos. More than that, I wish I had been able to get a job at Los Alamos or the university. Me, and half of Albuquerque.

Sherie comes home, her hair rough-cut in her kitchen with a mirror. She is loud and comfortable. Her belly is just a gentle insistent curve under her blue Rumatel goat dewormer T-shirt. Brenda hangs on her every word, knows about the trials and tribulations of raising goats, asks about Ed and the truck. She feeds us lunch.

I thought this life of thoughtful liberalism was my birthright, too. Before I understood that my generation was to be born in interesting times.

At the obstetrician's office, I sit in the waiting room and try not to fall asleep. I'm stuffed on Brenda's chicken-and-cheese sandwich and corn chowder. *People* magazine has an article about Tom Cruise getting telomerase regeneration therapy, which will extend his lifespan an additional forty years. There's an article on some music guy's house talking about the new opulence: cutting-edge technology that darkens the windows at the touch of a hand and walls that change color, rooms that sense whether you're warm or cold and change their temperature, and his love of ancient Turkish and Russian antiques. There's an article on a woman who has dedicated her life to helping people in Siberia who have AIDS.

Sherie comes out of the doctor's office on her cellphone. The doctor tells her that if she had insurance, they'd do a routine ultrasound. I can hear half the conversation as she discusses it with her mother. "This little guy," Sherie says, hand on her belly, "is half good Chinese peasant stock. He's doing fine." They decide to wait for another month.

Sherie is convinced that it's a boy. Ed is convinced it's a girl. He sings David Bowie's "China Girl" to Sherie's stomach, which for some reason irritates the hell out of her.

We stop on our way out of town and stock up on rice and beans, flour, sugar, coffee. We can get all this in Belen, but it's cheaper at Sam's Club. Sherie has a membership. I pay half the membership, and she uses the card to buy all our groceries, then I pay her back when we get to the car. The cashiers surely know that we're sharing a membership, but they don't care.

It's a long, hot drive back home. The air conditioning doesn't work in the truck. I am so grateful to see the trees that mark the valley.

My front door is standing open.

"Who's here?" Sherie says.

Abby is standing in the front yard, and she has clearly recognized Sherie's truck. She's barking her fool head off and wagging her tail, desperate. She runs to the truck. I get out and head for the front door, and she runs toward the door and then back toward me and then toward the door, unwilling to go in until I get there, then lunging through the door ahead of me.

"Hudson?" I call the other dog, but I know if the door is open, he's out roaming. Lost. My things are strewn everywhere, couch cushions on the floor, my kitchen drawers emptied on the floor, the back door open. I go through to the back, calling the missing dog, hoping against hope he is in the back yard. The back gate is open, too.

Behind me I hear Sherie calling, "Don't go in there by yourself!"

"My dog is gone," I say.

"Hudson?" she says.

I go out the back and call for him. There's no sign of him. He's a great boy, but some dogs, like Abby, tend to stay close to home. Hudson isn't one of those dogs.

Sherie and I walk through the house. No one is there. I go out to my workshop. My toolbox is gone, but evidently whoever did this didn't see the computer closed and sitting on the shelf just above eye level.

It had to be the guy I gave soup to. He probably went nearby to wait out the heat of the day and saw me leave.

I close and lock the gate, and the workshop. Close and lock my back door. Abby clings to me. Dogs don't like things to be different.

"We'll look for him," Sherie says. Abby and I climb into the truck, and for an hour we drive back roads, looking and calling, but there's no sign of him. Her husband, Ed, calls us. He's called the county and there's a deputy at my place waiting to take a statement. We walk through the house, and I identify what's gone. As best I can tell, it isn't much. Just the tools, mainly. The sheriff says they are usually looking for money, guns, jewelry. I had all my cards and my cell phone with me, and all my jewelry is inexpensive stuff. I don't have a gun.

I tell the deputy about the migrant this morning. He says it could have been him, or someone else. I get the feeling we'll never know. He promises to put out the word about the dog.

It is getting dark when they all leave, and I put the couch cushions on the couch. I pick up silverware off the floor and run hot water in the sink to wash it all. Abby stands at the back door, whining, but doesn't want to go out alone.

It occurs to me suddenly that the doll I was working on is missing. He stole the doll. Why? He's not going to be able to sell it. To send it home, I guess, to the baby in the photo. Or maybe to his wife, who has a real baby and is undoubtedly feeling a lot less sentimental about infants than most of my customers do. It's a couple of weeks of work, not full time, but painting, waiting for the paint to cure, painting again.

Abby whines again. Hudson is out there in the dark. Lost dogs don't do well in the desert. There are rattlesnakes. I didn't protect him. I sit down on the floor and wrap my arms around Abby's neck and cry. I'm a stupid woman who is stupid about my dogs, I know. But they are what I have.

I don't really sleep. I hear noises all night long. I worry about what I am going to do about money.

Replacing the tools is going to be a problem. The next morning I put the first layer of paint on a new doll to replace the stolen one. Then I do something I have resisted doing. Plastic doll parts aren't the only thing I can mold and sell on the internet. I start a clay model for a dildo. Over the last couple of years I've gotten queries from companies who have seen the dolls online and asked if I would consider doing dildos for them. Realistic penises aren't really any more difficult to carve than realistic baby hands. Easier, actually. I can't send it to Tony; he wouldn't do dildos. But a few years ago they came out with room-temperature, medical-grade silicone. I can make my own molds, do small runs, hand finish them. Make them as perfectly lifelike as the dolls. I can hope people will pay for novelty when it comes to sex.

I don't particularly like making doll parts, but I don't dislike it, either. Dildos, on the other hand, just make me sad. I don't think there is anything wrong with using them, it's not that. It's just … I don't know. I'm not going to stop making dolls, I tell myself.

I also email the Chicago couple back and accept the commission for the special, to make the same doll for the third time. Then I take a break and clean my kitchen some more. Sherie calls me to check how I'm doing, and I tell her about the dildos. She laughs. "You should have done it years ago," she says. "You'll be rich."

I laugh, too. And I feel a little better when I finish the call.

I try not to think about Hudson. It's well over a hundred today. I don't want to think about him in trouble, without water. I try to concentrate on penile veins. On the stretch of skin underneath the head (I'm making a circumcised penis). When my cell rings, I jump.

The guy on the phone says, "I've got a dog here, he's got this number on his collar. You missing a dog?"

"A golden retriever?" I say.

"Yep."

"His name is Hudson," I say. "Oh, thank you. Thank you. I'll be right there."

I grab my purse. I've got fifty-five dollars in cash. Not much of a reward, but all I can do. "Abby!" I yell. "Come on, girl! Let's go get Hudson!"

She bounces up from the floor, clueless, but excited by my voice.

"Go for a ride?" I ask.

We get in my ancient red Impreza. It's not too reliable, but we aren't going far. We bump across miles of bad road, most of it unpaved, following the GPS directions on my phone, and end up at a trailer in the middle of nowhere. It's bleached and surrounded by trash—an old easy chair, a kitchen chair lying on its side with one leg broken and the white unstained inside like a scar, an old picnic table. There's a dirty green cooler and a bunch of empty forty ounce bottles. Frankly, if I saw the place, my assumption would be that the owner made meth. But the old man who opens the door is just an old guy in a baseball cap. Probably living on social security.

"I'm Nick," he says. He's wearing a long-sleeved plaid shirt, despite the heat. He's deeply tanned and has a turkey-wattle neck.

I introduce myself. Point to the car and say, "That's Abby, the smart one that stays home."

The trailer is dark and smells of old man inside. The couch cushions are covered in cheap throws, one of them decorated with a blue-and-white Christmas snowman. Outside, the scrub shimmers, flattened in the heat. Hudson is lying in front of the sink and scrabbles up when he sees us.

"He was just ambling up the road," Nick says. "He saw me and came right up."

"I live over by the river, off 109, between Belen and Jarales," I say. "Someone broke into my place and left the doors open, and he wandered off."

"You're lucky they didn't kill the dogs," Nick says.

I fumble with my purse. "There's a reward," I say.

He waves that away. "No, don't you go starting that." He says he didn't do anything but read the tag and give him a drink. "I had dogs all my life," he says. "I'd want someone to call me."

I tell him it would mean a lot to me and press the money on him. Hudson leans against my legs to be petted, tongue lolling. He looks fine. No worse for wear.

"Sit a minute. You came all the way out here. Pardon the mess. My sister's grandson and his friends have been coming out here, and they leave stuff like that," he says, waving at the junk and the bottles.

"I can't leave the other dog in the heat," I say, wanting to leave.

"Bring her inside."

I don't want to stay, but I'm grateful, so I bring Abby in out of the heat, and he thumps her and tells me about how he's lived here since he was in his twenties. He's a Libertarian, and he doesn't trust government, and he really doesn't trust the New Mexico state government which is, in his estimation, a banana republic lacking only the fancy uniforms that third-world dictators seem to love. Then he tells me about how lucky it was that Hudson didn't get picked up to be a bait dog for the people who raise dogs for dogfights. Then he tells me about how the American economy was destroyed by operatives from Russia as revenge for the fall of the Soviet Union.

Half of what he says is bullshit and the other half is wrong, but he's just a lonely guy in the middle of the desert, and he brought me back my dog. The least I can do is listen.

I hear a spitting little engine off in the distance. Then a couple of them. It's the little motorbikes the kids ride. Nick's eyes narrow as he looks out.

"It's my sister's grandson," he says. "Goddamn."

He gets up, and Abby whines. He stands, looking out the slatted blinds.

"Goddamn. He's got a couple of friends," Nick says. "Look you just get your dogs and don't say nothing to them, okay? You just go on."

"Hudson," I say and clip a lead on him.

Outside, four boys pull into the yard, kicking up dust. They have seen my car and are obviously curious. They wear jumpsuits like prison jumpsuits, only with the sleeves ripped off and the legs cut off just above the knees. Khaki and orange and olive green. One of them has tattoos swirling up his arms.

"Hey, Nick," the tattooed one says, "new girlfriend?"

"None of your business, Ethan."

The boy is dark, but his eyes are light blue. Like a Siberian husky. "You a social worker?" the boy says.

"I told you it was none of your business," Nick says. "The lady is just going."

"If you're a social worker, you should know that old Nick is crazy, and you can't believe nothing he says."

One of the other boys says, "She isn't a social worker. Social workers don't have dogs."

I step down the steps and walk to my car. The boys sit on their bikes, and I have to walk around them to get to the Impreza. Hudson wants to see them, pulling against his leash, but I hold him in tight.

"You look nervous, lady," the tattooed boy says.

"Leave her alone, Ethan," Nick says.

"You shut up, Uncle Nick, or I'll kick your ass," the boy says absently, never taking his eyes off me.

Nick says nothing.

I say nothing. I just get my dogs in my car and drive away.

Our life settles into a new normal. I get a response from my dildo email. Nick in Montana is willing to let me sell on his sex site on commission. I make a couple of different models, including one that I paint just as realistically as I would one of the reborn dolls. This means a base coat, then I paint the veins in. Then I bake it. Then I paint an almost translucent layer of color and bake it again. Six layers. And then a clear overlayer of silicone because I don't think the paint is approved for use this way. I put a pretty hefty price on it and call it a special. At the same time, I am making my other special. The doll for the Chicago couple. I sent the mold to Tony and had him do a third head from it. It, too, requires layers of paint, and sometimes the parts bake side by side.

Because my business is rather slow, I take more time than usual. I am always careful, especially with specials. I think if someone is going to spend the kind of money one of these costs, the doll should be made to the best of my ability. And maybe it is because I have done this doll before, it comes easily and well. I think of the doll that the man who broke into my house stole. I don't know if he sent it to his wife and daughter in Mexico, or if he even has a wife and daughter in Mexico. I rather suspect he sold it on eBay or some equivalent—although I have watched doll sales and never seen it come up.

This doll is my orphan doll. She is full of sadness. She is inhabited by the loss of so much. I remember my fear when Hudson was wandering the roads of the desert. I imagine Rachel Mazar, so haunted by the loss of her own child. The curves of the doll's tiny fists are porcelain pale. The blue veins at her temples are traceries of the palest of bruises.

When I am finished with her, I package her as carefully as I have ever packaged a doll and send her off.

My dildos go up on the website.

The realistic dildo sits in my workshop, upright, tumescent, a beautiful rosy plum color. It sits on a shelf like a prize, glistening in its topcoat as if it were wet. It was surprisingly fun to make, after years and years of doll parts. It sits there both as an object to admire and as an affront. But, to be frank, I don't think it is any more immoral than the dolls. There is something straightforward about a dildo. Something much more clear than a doll made to look like a dead child. Something significantly less entangled.

There are no orders for dildos. I lie awake at night thinking about real-estate taxes. My father is dead. My mother lives in subsidized housing for the elderly in Columbus. I haven't been to see her in years and years, not with the cost of a trip like that. My car wouldn't make it, and nobody I know can afford to fly anymore. I certainly couldn't live with her. She would lose her housing if I moved in.

If I lose my house to unpaid taxes, do I live in my car? It seems like the beginning of the long slide. Maybe Sherie and Ed would take the dogs.

I do get a reprieve when the money comes in for the special. Thank God for the Mazars in Chicago. However crazy their motives, they pay promptly and by internet, which allows me to put money against the equity line for the new tools.

I still can't sleep at night, and instead of putting all the money against my debt, I put the minimum, and I buy a 9 mm handgun. Actually, Ed buys it for me. I don't even know where to get a gun.

Sherie picks me up in the truck and brings me over to the goat farm. Ed has several guns. He has an old gun safe that belonged to his father. When we get to their place, he is in back, putting creosote on new fence posts, but he is happy to come up to the house.

"So, you've given in," he says, grinning. "You've joined the dark side."

"I have," I agree.

"Well, this is a decent defensive weapon," Ed says. Ed does not fit my preconceived notions of a gun owner. Ed fits my preconceived notions of the guy who sells you a cell phone at the local strip mall. His hair is short and graying. He doesn't look at all like the kind of guy who would either marry Sherie or raise goats. He told me one time that his degree is in anthropology. Which, he said, was a difficult field to get a job in.

"Offer her a cold drink!" Sherie yells from the bathroom. In her pregnant state, Sherie can't ride twenty minutes in the sprung-shocked truck without having to pee.

He offers me iced tea and then gets the gun, checks to see that it isn't loaded, and hands it to me. He explains to me that the first thing I should do is check to see if the gun is loaded.

"You just did," I say.

"Yeah," he says, "but I might be an idiot. It's a good thing to do." He shows me how to check the gun.

It is not nearly so heavy in my hand as I thought it would be. But, truthfully, I have found that the thing you thought would be life changing so rarely is.

Later he takes me around to the side yard and shows me how to load and shoot it. I am not even remotely surprised that it is kind of fun. That is exactly what I expected.

———

Out of the blue, an email from Rachel Mazar of Chicago.

I am writing you to ask you if you have had any personal or business dealings with my husband, Ellam Mazar. If I do not get a response from you, your next correspondence will be from my attorney.

I don't quite know what to do. I dither. I make vegetarian chili. Oddly enough, I check my gun, which I keep in the bedside drawer. I am not sure what I am going to do about the gun when Sherie has her baby. I have offered to babysit, and I'll have to lock it up, I think. But that seems to defeat the purpose of having it.

While I am dithering, my cell rings. It is, of course, Rachel Mazar.

"I need you to explain your relationship with my husband, Ellam Mazar," she says. She sounds educated, with that eradication of regional accent that signifies a decent college.

"My relationship?" I say.

"Your email was on his phone," she says, frostily.

I wonder if he is dead. The way she says it sounds so final. "I didn't know your husband," I say. "He just bought the dolls."

"Bought what?" she says.

"The dolls," I say.

"Dolls?" she says.

"Yes," I say.

"Like ... sex dolls?"

"No," I say. "Dolls. Reborns. Handmade dolls."

She obviously has no idea what I am talking about, which opens a world of strange possibilities in my mind. The dolls don't have orifices. Fetish objects? I tell her my website, and she looks it up.

"He ordered specials," I say.

"But these cost a couple of thousand dollars," she says.

A week's salary for someone like Ellam Mazar, I suspect. I envision him as a professional, although, frankly, for all I know he works in a dry-cleaning shop or something.

"I thought they were for you," I say. "I assumed you had lost a child. Sometimes people who have lost a child order one."

"We don't have children," she says. "We never wanted them." I can hear how stunned she is in the silence. Then she says, "Oh, my God."

Satanic rituals? Some weird abuse thing?

"That woman said he told her he had lost a child," she says.

I don't know what to say, so I just wait.

"My husband ... my soon-to-be-ex-husband," she says. "He has apparently been having affairs. One of the women contacted me. She told me that he told her we had a child that died and that now we were married in name only."

I hesitate. I don't know if legally I am allowed to tell her about transactions I had with her husband. On the other hand, the emails came with both their names on them. "He has bought three," I say.

"Three?"

"Not all at once. About once a year. But people who want a special send me a picture. He always sends the same picture."

"Oh," she says. "That's Ellam. He's orderly. He's used the same shampoo for fifteen years."

"I thought it was strange," I say. I can't bear not to ask. "What do you think he did with them?"

"I think the twisted bastard used them to make women feel sorry for him," she says through gritted teeth. "I think he got all sentimental about them. He probably has himself half convinced that he really did have a daughter. Or that it's my fault that we didn't have children. He never wanted children. Never."

"I think a lot of my customers like the idea of having a child better than having one," I say.

"I'm sure," she says. "Thank you for your time and I'm sorry to have bothered you."

So banal. So strange and yet so banal. I try to imagine him giving the doll to a woman, telling her that it was the image of his dead child. How did that work?

Orders for dildos begin to trickle in. I get a couple of doll orders and make a payment on the credit line and put away some toward real-estate taxes. I may not have to live in my car.

One evening, I am working in the garden when Abby and Hudson start barking at the back gate.

I get off my knees, aching, but lurch into the house and into the bedroom where I grab the 9 mm out of the bedside table. It isn't loaded, which now seems stupid. I try to think if I should stop and load it. My hands are shaking. It is undoubtedly just someone looking for a meal and a place to recharge. I decide I can't trust myself to load, and besides, the dogs are out there. I go to the back door, gun held stiffly at my side, pointed to the ground.

There are, in fact, two of them, alike as brothers, Indian looking with a fringe of black hair cut in a straight line above their eyebrows.

"Lady," one says, "we can work for food?" First one, then the other sees the gun at my side, and their faces go empty.

The dogs cavort.

"I will give you something to eat, and then you go," I say.

"We go," the one who spoke says.

"Someone robbed me," I say.

"We no rob you," he says. His eyes are on the gun. His companion takes a step back, glancing at the gate and then at me as if to gauge if I will shoot him if he bolts.

"I know," I say. "But someone came here, I gave him food, and he robbed me. You tell people not to come here, okay?"

"Okay," he says. "We go."

"Tell people not to come here," I say. I would give them something to eat, something to take with them. I hate this. They are two young men in a foreign country, hungry, looking for work. I could easily be sleeping in my car. I could be homeless. I could be wishing for someone to be nice to me.

But I am not. I'm just afraid.

"Hudson! Abby!" I yell, harsh, and the two men flinch. "Get in the house."

The dogs slink in behind me, not sure what they've done wrong.

"If you want some food, I will give you something," I say. "Tell people not to come here."

I don't think they understand me. Instead they back slowly away a handful of steps and then turn and walk quickly out the gate, closing it behind them.

I sit down where I am standing, knees shaking.

The moon is up in the blue early evening sky. Over my fence I can see scrub and desert, a fierce land where mountains breach like the petrified spines of apocalyptic animals. The kind of landscape that seems right for crazed gangs of mutants charging around in cobbled-together vehicles. Tribal remnants of America, their faces painted, their hair braided, wearing jewelry made from shiny CDs and cigarette lighters scrounged from the ruins of civilization. The desert is Byronic in its extremes.

I don't see the two men. There's no one out there in furs, their faces painted blue, driving a dune buggy built out of motorcycle parts and hung with the skulls of their enemies. There's just a couple of guys from Nicaragua or Guatemala, wearing T-shirts and jeans.

And me, sitting watching the desert go dark, the moon rising, an empty handgun in my hand.

The Lost Boy:
A Reporter At Large

On June 13, 2014, Simon Weiss came into the mechanic's shop where he worked in Brookneal, Virginia. He was a quiet kid in Carhartts overalls. He had started working at Brookneal Goodyear two years before, at sixteen. He was enrolled at the vocational school and living with a foster family. His auto mechanics teacher had found him the job after school. In the aftermath of the Baltimore attack, Brookneal had taken in more than its share of Baltimore homeless. Jim Dwyer, who owns Brookneal Goodyear, said that some of those people were problems. "A lot of those people were not used to working for a living," Dwyer says. "They expected to go on in Brookneal pretty much the way they had in Baltimore. I guess a lot of them had drug problems and such." But not Simon. He never missed work. He was always on time. Dwyer thought that work was the place Simon felt most comfortable. On Saturdays while he was still in high school, Simon arrived early in his lovingly maintained '08 Honda Civic. He made coffee and read the funnies while waiting for everyone else to arrive. He looked up to Dwyer and had asked Dwyer advice about a girl. The girl hadn't lasted. His foster parents were, in Dwyer's words, "decent people" but they had two other foster kids, one of whom had leukemia from the effects of the dirty bomb.

On this hot summer Friday morning, two weeks after Simon's graduation from high school, a couple came in at about 9:30 and asked to see Simon. There was something about them that made Dwyer watch closely when Simon came in from the back where he was doing an oil change. "When he came through that door," Dwyer said, "his expression never changed. He thought it was something about a car, someone complaining or asking a question or something, you could tell. He had a kind of polite expression on his face. But there wasn't a flash of recognition or anything. There was nothing."

When the woman saw him, she started sobbing. She called him William. He looked at Dwyer and then at her and said, "Okay." She was his mother, and she had been looking for him for five years.

"Why didn't you try to find us?" she asked.

"I don't remember," Simon said. And then he walked back into the garage, to the Lexus he was doing the oil change on. Dwyer followed him back. Simon did not respond when Dwyer spoke to him. He stood there for a moment, and then he started to cry. "I'm crazy," he told Dwyer.

When I met Simon, I asked him what he wanted me to call him. He shrugged and said most people called him Simon.

"Is that your name, now?" I asked.

"I guess," he said.

He was tired of talking about himself, he said. Tired of talking about his family and Baltimore. He was a quiet, passive kid, dressed in an oversized shirt. He answered my questions but didn't volunteer anything. We were meeting in a park, sitting at a picnic table. His car, a gold Civic, was parked not far away. It was impeccably maintained and had a handsome set of aftermarket wheels and some "mods." I admired it and said that I had a Civic in the '90s.

Simon murmered something polite.

I said it was the first car I ever bought with my own money. I lived in New York, I explained, and didn't own a car until I was thirty. But I had moved, and I loved that car.

He looked at me, nodding. I said I liked his wheels, which was true. They were in keeping with the car, not too flashy, I said.

In minutes I had learned the history of the car. Hands waving, he talked about how he saved for the wheels. We talked about the joys of spending a couple of hours really cleaning a car and the relative merits of different ways to clean interiors. I had assumed that the diffident young man was Simon. That this was the affect of someone with a problem. Instead, what I had found was a shy but normal boy who was not comfortable talking to a journalist. I am accustomed to people being wary of being interviewed, but I had forgotten that with Simon.

I had done research on memory loss like Simon's. It's called Dissociative fugue. Like most psychological diagnosis, it probably says as much about our culture as it does about Simon. I had expected someone in a mental fog and had projected that onto him.

Amnesia is a relatively common phenomenon, but mostly it's transient. Anyone who has ever been in a car wreck and can't remember the moment of the accident has experienced amnesia. But contrary to its popularity in movies and television, it is rare for a person to forget who they are.

Dissociative fugue is a condition where a person leaves home for hours, sometimes months. They have no memory of who they are and sometimes adopts another identity.

Two months after the Reverend Ansel Bourne disappeared from his home in Providence in January 1887, his nephew got a telegram telling him that a man in Norristown, PA, was acting strangely and claiming to be Ansel Bourne. Six weeks before, a man calling himself A. Brown had opened a fruit and candy store. He was normal, rather quiet. He cooked his meals in the back of his shop. One day Ansel Bourne "woke up" and found himself in a strange town. He had no memory of A. Brown and no idea where he was.

William James hypnotized Ansel Bourne and was able to call forth "A. Brown." A. Brown had never heard of Ansel Bourne. He complained that he felt "hedged in at both ends" because he could remember nothing before opening his shop and nothing from the time Ansel Bourne had woken up. Why had he come to Norristown? He said "there was trouble back there" and "he wanted rest."

Ansel Bourne's case perfectly fit the psychoanalytic category of hysteria, a diagnosis that was prevalent at the turn of the twentieth century but which has largely disappeared. He was a very intellectual man with high standards for behavior, who had disassociated himself from a life that exhausted him and picked up a different life. Bourne, it was said, had a strong aversion to trade. The personality of Brown was a shrunken version of Bourne.

Today we can surmise that starting a store from scratch, traveling to Philadelphia to establish suppliers, joining a new community, and learning a new town may not be 'simpler' than the intellectual life of a well-off, comfortable reverend. Like my assumptions about Simon, William James's analysis of Ansel Bourne includes unexamined assumptions about class and personality.

Simon took me for a ride in his Civic (which was far better maintained than mine ever had been). He was a good driver. He was interested in autocross and was saving money to take a class. I'm no judge of drivers, but I would say he had a natural feel for driving. While we were driving around the park, I asked him if he felt as if William was a different person.

"No," he said. "I'm William, too."

"Does it make you feel odd to be called William?" I asked.

He nodded, concentrating as he took a turn. "If people are calling me William, then Brookneal feels, you know, kind of not real. But if people are calling me Simon, then I can not worry about that."

"Do you ever think about Pikesville?" I asked.

"I don't like to," he said. And then the conversation turned back to cars.

Dissociative fugue is most common after some sort of trauma. It is mostly likely to occur after combat or natural disaster. It is assumed that the events in Baltimore triggered William/Simon's fugue. It is just not known exactly what happened to him. Or why, unlike most people, after a few hours or a few days, or, at most, a few weeks, he didn't tell someone his real name or seek his family out.

Luz Anitas Weil, William's mother, was at work when two dirty bombs exploded in Baltimore. A divorced mother of three, she lived in Pikesville, a suburb north and west of Baltimore. The Weils were not the typical Pikesville family. Hispanics make up about one percent of the student population. They're outnumbered by whites, blacks, and Asians. Luz had hung on in Pikesville after her divorce because she thought that her kids would get a better education there. More important, she thought they would grow up thinking middle class. Luz grew up in Belton, Texas. Her father runs a landscaping company. She met Nick Weil when he was stationed at Fort Hood. They were engaged in six weeks, married in nine months. Luz says, "We partied pretty hard. I was a wild child. We drank too much. We had big fights. I gave as good as I got." After two and a half more years, Nick Weil was discharged and they returned to Maryland. Soon after, Luz got pregnant and had William. She shrugs. "After William was born, I stopped partying. I stopped drinking. Nick didn't. That's when I realized his hitting me, that wasn't us fighting, that was abuse." They tried going to counseling. A second boy, Robert, was born two years after William. After that, they were separated for two years and got back together instead of divorcing, and seven years after William, Inez was born. But by then Luz says she knew it was over, and they were divorced soon after.

She got a job working in the kitchen at the Woodholme Country Club. Fancy dinners for fancy people. It was the first place in Maryland where she was around people speaking Spanish. Like a lot of restaurants and kitchens, most of the help was from Central America. But they were men and they didn't have much patience with a Texas-born Latina. "Every day I had to prove myself again," Luz said. Which she did, moving up until she was catering. "You know, thirty-thousand-dollar weddings, where everything has to be just right." She liked the work, except for the hours, which, she felt, kept her away from her kids too much. When someone came into the kitchen that Friday afternoon and said, "There's been a bomb," she says she didn't understand. "I thought they meant that there had been a bomb at Woodholme. The first thing I thought was that I didn't hear anything, you know? I thought it couldn't be that big a deal." Normally, William, then 13, would have been home with his brother and sister—Robert, 11 and Inez, 6. William was the oldest and had just that year turned old enough to babysit. Child care was expensive, and having a child old enough to watch the other two was making a huge difference. But William was at the Maryland Science Museum in the IMAX Theater with his seventh-grade class. They were watching *Andean Condors, Lords of the High Reaches* when the first bomb exploded across the harbor in Patterson Park. The wind from the northwest pushed the plume south and east across Dundalk, away from Harborplace and the museums.

William's classmates say he was there at the IMAX, but no one knows what happened next. William says he doesn't remember. For the famous fifty-one minutes when no one knew the bomb was a dirty bomb and that radioactive materials were being dispersed in the plume, William's class continued to enjoy the museum. Several boys got in trouble for getting each other wet with an exhibit and then a drinking fountain. The first indication that there was any trouble was when the museum announced that they would be closing. It was 2:35. Cell phones started ringing with parents checking on their children. At 2:42, the second bomb exploded near the Baltimore Washington International Airport. By the time the buses were rolling for Pikesville, roads were already congested.

William wasn't on his bus.

No one knows what happened or how he got separated. Teachers did counts and called attendance, but it was pretty chaotic. Kids were on cell phones and not paying attention. Children were crying. Teachers were trying to check on their own families. The cell phone system was completely overloaded, and people couldn't get anything beyond the "circuits are busy" message. Luz was trying to call William and getting no answer.

Luz was at the school with Robert and Inez in the car when the buses got to Pikesville Middle School. The car was packed with clothes, photo albums, and the cat, Splinter. Luz says she waited with growing dread as the buses emptied and left, one by one. When William didn't get off with his classmates, she told herself he was on another bus. But eventually, all the busses were emptied. She went and found the assistant principal and told him that William hadn't gotten off. The assistant principal assumed that she had just missed him in the crowd, and they searched inside the school.

But he had children, and he was desperate to get home and maybe get them out of the city. Luz tried to drive downtown and was turned back by police. "I told them that I had to find my boy," she says, and the tears well up. "They told me that I couldn't go any farther, that the city was contaminated. They said people were helping anyone left behind." She tried to insist, but a policeman finally said to her that she had more than one child to think about, and did she want to expose the other two?

She turned the car around and drove north, joining the slow crawl of vehicles out of Baltimore. Her plan was to find a safe place for the other two kids and then turn back. She ran out of gas in Dillsburg, Pennsylvania. A passing motorist stopped and called police for advice, and she and the two children were taken to a school gymnasium that had been turned into a shelter. There, a volunteer (a member of the VFW) passed a Geiger counter over her and the two children, gave them sheets and blankets, and directed them toward cots. It was two more days before she could find someone to give her a ride to a gas station and then back to her car. She drove back to Baltimore but was again turned away, this time with instructions to contact the Red Cross. She did contact the Red Cross, but they had no mention of William. For the next week she made the hour-and-a-half trip to Baltimore every day, only to be turned away.

Finally, there was simply no more money for gas.

There is something compelling about the idea of someone who has lost their memory. It taps into an almost universal desire to wipe the slate clean, to start over. In fiction and in film, it is often a chance for a person to redeem themselves.

Doug Bruce walked into a Coney Island police station on July 3, 2003, and said that he didn't know who he was or where he lived. He had woken up on the subway without wallet or identification. He could speak, he had skills—since he knew how to swim before he lost his memory, he still knew how. But he could not remember ever having seen the ocean. He couldn't remember family or friends. Police found a phone number in a knapsack that Bruce was wearing, and a friend came and picked him up. He was a stockbroker with a loft, cockatoos, and a dog. He became a cause célèbre, in no small part because he was so charmed by the world. Everything was new. It was his first rain, his first snow, his first exposure to the Rolling Stones, his first shop window. Friends said that before he lost his memory, he was somewhat arrogant, and that afterward he was much more … delightful.

He has never had MRIs, which would go a long way toward verifying whether or not he has amnesia (recall of memories cause certain kinds of visible brain activity), and there is considerable doubt as to whether or not he is lying. Complete retrograde amnesia, the kind of amnesia Doug Bruce claims to have, is extraordinarily rare. It rarely persists for more than a few months. In 2005, Bruce was the subject of a documentary called *Unknown White Male*. After it was released, he stopped giving interviews.

A boy with no identification but who said his name was Simon Weiss was found on the streets of downtown Baltimore five days after the bombs exploded. He was hungry and mildly dehydrated, but he had obviously eaten and drunk during the five days. He was brought to a Red Cross relief center, where his name was entered in a data bank for missing persons. When he was asked where his family was, he said he didn't know. He was asked his mother's name and said he didn't know. Area hospitals were still overwhelmed with people who had been, or thought they had been, exposed to radioactive waste from the bombs. His file was marked for follow-up with a psychologist and he was transported to the refugee center outside Richmond, Virginia.

A number of refugees were moved to the Virginia National Guard station at Fort Pickett and put in barracks-style housing. The boy who called himself Simon was there for five months.

"Yeah, I remember it," he said. "It wasn't so bad. Boring. I watched a lot of television. I had never seen *Lost*, so I watched the whole thing from beginning to end in reruns. They were showing two episodes a day from 9:00 to 11:00. I remember that. And then one night I saw the *Simpsons* where they did the last episode about *Lost*, where they all get rescued, and they mixed *Gilligan's Island* in with it, and Homer Simpson was the old guy, the Skipper." His face crinkled with laughter. He was animated. He was present in the memory. Asked about what he remembered from before Fort Pickett, he described the Red Cross worker who asked him questions—a somewhat scary lady with gray hair, he said. Asked about before that and his face changed, went oddly slack.

"Do you remember going to school in Pikesville?"

"Yeah," he said. Pressed for what he remembers. he said, "The monkey bars." He shrugged. Looked away.

Eventually, when no one came forward to claim him, Simon Weiss was placed in the foster-care system and ended up with a family in Brookneal. (The family did not want to be identified in this article.)

Jim Dwyer, the mechanic whom the boy eventually came to work for, believes that there is a reason that he doesn't remember. "I don't know exactly what happened," Dwyer says, "but something obviously wasn't right with the family." He won't be pinned down, but the implication is he suspects abuse or at least neglect. He believes that the boy separated mentally and emotionally.

Luz, Robert (now 16), and Inez (now 11) deny that there was abuse. "We were never abused," Robert says. "I don't know who said that, but it's not true."

Robert is a soft-spoken boy who remembers William as "a great kid. A great older brother." He remembers that William was the one whom their mother left in charge sometimes, but until that last year, he says, they always had a babysitter. Inez has memories, but they are more vague. What she remembers better is the home after Baltimore. "We were always hearing about William," she says. "About where he might be. Mom was always calling someone because of something on the internet or on television."

No one but Luz and the children believed that William was alive. There are about a hundred people who have never been accounted for, and it was assumed that William had either been killed during the bombing or had died in the day after. Luz moved them back to Pikesville as soon as they were able, in case William was looking for them. In the year before the Woodholme Country Club took her back, she worked a series of jobs. The kids remember going to a school that was mostly empty, so few people came back. There is no doubt that William's disappearance affected the family both financially and emotionally. Robert had nightmares, and Inez wet the bed. Both were afraid that things were contaminated. Inez got food poisoning from a hot dog and refused to eat for days. Even now, she is in therapy once a week because she is afraid to eat.

Luz was haunted by the fear that William had been exposed to radiation and was sick. The amount of radiation in the bombs was small, and it dispersed in plumes that trailed south and east, nowhere near Pikesville. She obsessively tracked down as much information as she could about the dispersal of the contaminants. She knew that William's school trip should not have exposed him (and it didn't), but she wondered if he had left the museum for some reason. She couldn't understand, if he wasn't sick, why he hadn't shown up on a list of displaced persons, somewhere.

But she couldn't give up. Finally, a relief worker found a list of children who had been placed in foster homes and gave Luz the number of the social worker who had Simon's case. The social worker wasn't sure that Simon and William were the same person, but she gave Luz the phone number of the foster parents. That was on Friday. I asked Luz if she called right away.

"I couldn't," she admits. "I started thinking, 'Why didn't he call us? What's wrong?' I thought that it couldn't be him. I thought a thousand things. I thought he was angry because I hadn't come and gotten him." The next morning she put the kids in the car, and they drove to Brookneal where she rang the doorbell of the foster parents. They sent her to Simon's job.

"I did it all wrong," she says. "I should have called him. I didn't know about the memory thing. I thought maybe something had happened to him, that he had been hurt or abused or … I didn't know."

But she had to make the trip. Had to see him. She didn't know what she would do if it was William and he didn't want to see them. "When we in Pennsylvania and I kept driving back, trying to get into Baltimore to look for him, every time I got to a barricade and they turned me around, I felt as if William thought I was abandoning him.

I wasn't going to abandon him. I promised him every night, lying in bed, I would not give up. I would find him." She looks fierce. "And I did."

Finally in therapy, Simon/William was unable to talk much about either his life in Brookneal or his life in Pikesville. In the presence of his family, he became almost mute. It was too much. Something triggered the creation of Simon, but Stein Testchloff, an authority on Dissociative disorder at Cornell University Medical, says it didn't have to be either abuse or some terrible event in Baltimore—or, at least, nothing more terrible than getting separated from his class. It appears that some people are predisposed to disassociation. "When someone goes missing for weeks," he explains, "it usually turns out that they have experienced fugue states before, usually for only a couple of hours." Luz says that as far as she knows, William never forgot who he was and left home, but as Testchloff points out, William was young and may not have had a fugue experience before. But if he did have a predisposition toward fugue, then the fear and chaos of his experience in Baltimore could certainly have brought it on.

Usually the treatment for someone with dissociative fugue is to bring them out of the fugue state, but William Weir/Simon Weiss doesn't appear to be in a fugue. Testchloff says appearance can be deceiving. "We think of this as a dramatic thing, a kind of on/off switch. He was William, now he is Simon. But the brain can be much more fuzzy. I think after he's spent five years of living as Simon Weiss, it is going to be very difficult for him to bring those two histories together."

Testchloff feels that what has happened to William is close to Disassociative Identity Disorder (DID), which used to be called Multiple Personality. He is reluctant to make that statement, because there is so much misinformation about DID. "Everybody thinks *Sybil*," he says. But there is a lot of doubt about Sybil, and, again, everyone assumes it is like the movies—that the separate personalities don't leak over into each other—when in many cases, some personalities know all about other personalities, and there can be a kind of fluidity in which personalities merge and break apart. Again, popular literature and movies have given an impression that is perhaps less complicated than reality. Testchloff has not seen William and has only reviewed his chart (with the permission of William, his therapist, and his family). He says it seems that Simon now has memories of growing up in Pikesville, but there is some sense in which he has assigned all that to William and holds it at arm's length.

When asked what he wants, Simon says he wants to keep working for Jim Dwyer. Does he want to continue to see his family?

He does, although he expresses no enthusiasm.

What does he think of his family?

He looks shy. "They're nice," he says, almost too soft to hear. "I like them okay." Then, after a moment, "I always wished I would have a family."

(Shortly after this piece was written, Simon disappeared for seventy-two hours. He called Jim Dwyer from Norfolk, Virginia, saying he didn't know how he had gotten there. Dwyer drove to Norfolk and picked him up. Luz and Robert and Inez are still living in Pikesville, but they see William almost every weekend. He has plans to spend Thanksgiving with them.)

The Kingdom of the Blind

At 3:17 EST, the lights at DM Kensington Medical did the wave. Starting at the east end of the building, the lights went out and, after just a couple of seconds, came back on. The darkness went down the hall. Staff looked up. It was a local version of a rolling blackout, a kind of weird utility/weather event. In its wake, IV alarms went off, monitors re-set. Everything critical was on backup, but not everything was critical. Some of it was just important, and some of it wasn't even important, unless you consider coffee a life-or-death substance. Which, for a resident, might be true. It was not life-threatening in the immediate sense, but it wasn't trivial, and it interrupted two nurses and a resident working on a woman in ICU having seizures, a pharmacist counting meds, a CT scan, a couple of X-rays, and it derailed a couple of consultations. The line of darkness washed across the buildings, leapt the parking lot, split into two parts, and then washed north and south simultaneously across a complex of medical offices.

At 3:21, the same thing happened at UH Southpoint Medical. UH Southpoint was in Tennessee, and Kensington was in Texas. At 3:25 it rolled through Seattle Kellerman, although there it started in the north and went south. The three hospitals were all part of the Benevola Health Network. Their physical plant—thermostats, lights, hot water, and air filtration—were all handled by BHP DMS, a software system. Specifically, by a subroutine called SAMEDI. SAMEDI was not an acronym. It was the name of a Haitian Voodoo *loa*, a possession spirit. A lot of the subroutines in BHP DMS were named for Haitian *loa*. The system that monitored lab results and watched for emergent epidemiological trends (a fancy way of saying something that noticed if there were signs of, say, an upsurge in cases of West Nile virus, or an outbreak of food poisoning symptoms across several local ERs) was called LEGBA, after the guardian of the crossroads, the trickster who managed traffic between life and the spirit world. Some programmers had undoubtedly been very pleased with themselves.

The problem line lit up in BHP DMS IT.

"Sydney, phone," Damien said.

"You get it."

"You're the least Asperger's person in the department. It's that having two X chromosomes thing."

Actually, the only people in the department who were clinically Aspergers were probably Dale, who was a hardware guy, and their boss, Tony.

"In the kingdom of the blind," Sydney said. "The one-eyed girl is king."

"The difference between see/not see is a lot bigger than the difference between one eye and two eyes," Damien said.

Sydney picked up the phone. "Hi, this is Sydney." It was 4:49 EST, and the lights went out.

"Fuck," said Vahn, a couple of cubes down. "There goes two hours."

"Save early, save often," Dale said.

"Fuck. Fuck. Fuck."

The lights came back on, and everyone's systems started booting up.

"Hello?" said the voice on the phone.

"Sorry," Sydney said, "we just had a power glitch."

"Well, you and everyone else," said the man on the phone. "The system is screwy again."

The system had been screwy for months. Sydney thought someone had probably been messing with it, introducing bugs or maybe even writing some sort of virus. BHP DMS was an elaborate system. Sydney, Damien, and the ten other people who took care of BHP DMS actually worked for Cronaut Labs, the company that had put BHP DMS together. Cronaut contracted them to Benevola.

BHP DMS had been engineered by using genetic algorithms. Genetic algorithms weren't genetic, actually. Damien had had an AI class in college, and they had talked about genetic algorithms. Programmers wrote a couple of different programs that solved a particular problem. Then they wrote some code that chopped and recombined chunks of programs and generated hundreds of program offspring, most of which didn't work at all. They tested those programs by having them solve the problem, threw out the ones that didn't work, and did the same thing all over again with the programs that were left. The result was messy and full of odd quirks, but sometimes the results were more efficient than traditionally written code. It had a lot of apparent junk. Spaghetti code that made no sense. BHP DMS made a Microsoft operating system look elegant and streamlined, but it could do some amazingly complex stuff. Damien was really interested in genetic algorithms. He had written some stuff into SAMEDI so that he could have it run a report that output variables at different points. He had shown Sydney a place where SAMEDI seemed to be reading stuff in and out of memory for no particular reason.

"That's classic," he said. "It looks pointless. But I bet if you take it out, the program crashes."

In the last couple of months, BHP DMS subsystems had been crashing a lot.

Sydney was not really a code monkey the way Damien was. She had a degree in computer science, and she could write code, but she had come straight out of school into support. Damien had actually done programming for Threepoint Games. He had told her about the game-development death march to deadline, working eighteen-hour days in the crunch before release of their game, SphereGuardian, sleeping at work and living on cereal and Power Bars and caffeine. SphereGuardian had not been a success. In fact, it had sucked. The company had folded. Damien had ended up at Benevola "until he got a better job." That had been three years ago.

Sydney did not expect to get a better job, at least not in computers. She was pretty sure she had gotten this job because she was a woman, and human resources had seen an opportunity to increase diversity. Most of the guys had more experience than she did. But she had been getting a lot of experience in the last year. Big systems like BHP DMS could get buggy, and BHP DMS had, so they had all been writing what Sydney thought of as code boxes. A subsystem would start doing something weird—crashing a lot, although when it was restarted they couldn't find anything wrong. Then it would start doing something just plain weird, the way SAMEDI had just run the wave on the electrical systems. They would try to track down a point in the program where they could find something that triggered the event, and then they'd write some code to try to box that behavior in. Something that said, "when you want the electrical system to roll over that way, do this instead."

Sydney was not all that good at it. Which was one reason why she answered the phone. It was a way of being useful. She did a lot of grunt work for Damien. A lot of coding is dull as hell. Database-dull kind of stuff. Sydney got stuck with a lot of that. That was why she stood up and looked over the cube wall and said to Damien, "I figured out why it started with Kensington and then went to Southpoint."

Damien looked up at her. He was short, pale, with black hair. He was growing a goatee, and the hair was still sparse and wiry. But he had big, soulful-looking eyes which Sydney was beginning to suspect had caused her to attribute to Damien certain emotional characteristics—sensitivity, vulnerability—that he, in fact, did not have. But he was funny and fun to work with. On the wall of his cube was a poster for SphereGuardian showing a guy in a space suit that made him look like a large, red human-insect carrying a spiky-looking gun. Sydney had bought the game in the cheap rack for fifteen dollars. It had sucked.

"That's the order they're stacked in SAMEDI," she said. "There's a table."

"That's cool," Damien said.

Sydney waited a moment and, when Damien didn't say anything else, sat back down. Damien could get in the zone when he coded. He said hours could pass during which he forgot to eat. Didn't notice what time it was. He was not that skinny for a guy who could forget to eat. Sydney had never forgotten to eat in her life. One of her secret fantasies had been that, as a girl who could code, she would work in the one place where a geeky fat girl could get dates. It had not been entirely untrue. But as someone had pointed out to her in school, although the odds are good, the goods are odd.

Damien believed that BHP DMS was aware.

Sydney had found the *Wired* magazine article where he'd gotten the idea, although she'd never told him that; she'd gone along with the fiction that Damien had figured it out himself. In the last couple of years, a number of big complex systems had, like BHP DMS, gotten buggy and weird and had started crashing in inexplicable ways. Eventually, all four of the systems had been wiped and reestablished from two-year-old backups, and in three cases, the problems had stopped. In one case, after several months, the problems had started back up again.

The guy who wrote the article had interviewed a scientist at MIT who thought that the systems had shown patterns that seemed purposeful and that could be interpreted as signs that the systems were testing their environments. Since their "environments" were the complex fields of data inputted into them, they didn't see or hear or smell or taste. BHP DMS actually did monitor security cameras, smoke detectors, CO detectors, and a host of other machines, but it didn't care what the security cameras "saw." It checked them for orientation. It made sure that the smoke detectors had backup batteries with a charge. It didn't use them to sense the world; it sensed them.

Sydney stood back up and looked over the cubicle wall again. After a moment, Damien looked up at her.

"What do you think DMS wants?" she asked.

He looked puzzled. Or maybe he was really not paying attention to her. Sometimes when she interrupted him, he only appeared to be looking at her.

"If it's aware," she said. "What does it want?"

"Why does it have to want anything?" he asked.

"Everything wants something," Sydney said.

"Rocks don't want anything."

"Everything alive wants something," Sydney said.

Damien shook his head. "I didn't say it was alive. I said it was aware."

"How can you be aware but not alive?"

"Do you believe in life after death?"

Sydney did not believe in life after death, but in her experience, admitting this could lead to long and complicated discussions in which people seemed to think that since she did not believe in God or the afterlife, there was nothing to stop her from becoming an ax murderer. She was pretty sure that Damien didn't believe in God—he had a stridently pro-evolution T-shirt that said *EVOLUTION How can 100 bazillion antibiotic-resistant bacteria be wrong?*—but she wasn't absolutely certain. "A ghost or a spirit was alive," she said.

Damien shrugged and looked back at his monitor.

Which meant that Sydney should sit down, so she did.

After a minute Damien looked over her cube wall. His head was right above the Mardi Gras mask hung on her wall. She didn't particularly want to go to Mardi Gras, which seemed to be mostly about blond girls flashing their tits; she just liked masks.

"I think DMS is aware but not alive," Damien said.

"I don't even know what that means,"

"Nobody does," Damien said. Then he sat back down.

They decided to poke it. Or, rather, Damien did. Sydney pointed out that they didn't know what it would do if they poked it—it could crash, it could shut down all the electrical systems, it could delete all the pharmaceutical records from the previous year.

"Then we'll install from backup," Damien said. "We'll do it at 1:00 a.m. We'll send out a system maintenance bulletin." Hospitals don't shut down, but they do a lot less at 1:00 a.m.

Sydney said, "But if we install from backup, we'll be killing it."

Damien leaned back in his chair. "Ah, the old transporter question." They were sitting in his cube. His desk was a mess—stacked with papers, binders, a couple of manuals, and the remains of a dinner of Chinese food. "In *Star Trek*, if I beam you down to the planet, does that mean I have actually killed you and sent an exact replica in your place?"

"Yes," Sydney said. She was wearing her *If You're Really a Goth, Where Were You When We Sacked Rome?* T-shirt because Damien had laughed his ass off when she first wore it. Damien was wearing cut-off sweatpants and yellow flip-flops because even though the office was technically business casual, no one cared what you wore at 1:00 a.m. "Look, what if we shut it down, back it up, and it never comes back to consciousness?" She was thinking about the book *The Moon Is a Harsh Mistress* where the AI, Mike, is damaged during the war and after that never speaks again to Manny, the main character. Manny calls the secret phone number he has for Mike, but when he does, there is only silence. She'd read it when she was thirteen, and it had haunted

her. She told herself that eventually Mike "woke up" again and called
Manny.

"Why do you think it's conscious?" Damien said.

"Why do I think you're conscious?" Sydney said.

"You think I'm conscious because I'm like you, and you're conscious," Damien said. "DMS isn't like us."

"But if it's aware, then it has consciousness," Sydney said.

"Is a shark conscious?" Damien said.

"Yeah," Sydney said.

"How about a cricket? How about a jellyfish? A sponge?"

"If we don't know if DMS is conscious or not, then we pretty
much have to assume it is," Sydney said. "And if we back it up, we
might kill it."

Damien shook his head. "How can we kill it?"

Sydney said, "Because we will stop it and reinstall it."

"So you think that the interruption of consciousness might be
enough to kill it? You think it has a soul? Its consciousness is in the
code. Its code and body are unchanged. If someone has a heart attack
and you shock them back, they come back as themselves. Your body
is you. DMS's software and hardware is DMS." Damien was very
pleased with himself.

Sydney was pretty sure it wasn't so simple. It wasn't until the next
day that she thought of a cogent argument, which was that organic
systems are a lot less fragile than computer systems. Organic systems
decay gracefully. Computer systems break easily. DMS was much more
fragile than an animal. But that night she couldn't think of anything.

The problem with poking the system to see if it was aware was
to figure out what it could sense. DMS didn't see or hear, didn't eat
or breathe. Its "senses" were all involved in interpreting data. So the
"poke" needed to be something that it would recognize, that it would
sense. And the poke needed to be something that it would sense
as meaningful. The idea that Damien came up with was to feed it

information in a way that it could recognize was a pattern but that wasn't a pattern it expected.

DMS had several systems which regulated input and scanned for patterns. Epidemiological information was generated from ER, patient intake, and pharmaceutical information. Maintenance issues were anticipated from electrical usage. They picked the maintenance system, since DMS had been screwing with the electrical system, and input a thousand-character string of ones and zeroes. It was, Damien said, boring but clearly a pattern.

Sydney wasn't sure it was the right kind of pattern. "Basically," she said, "It's like I flipped a coin and it came up heads a thousand times."

"Yeah," Damien said.

"If I did that, I might assume there was something wrong with the coin. But I wouldn't assume aliens were trying to communicate with me through my coin toss."

"DMS doesn't have to recognize that we're trying to communicate with it," Damien explained. "It just has to notice that the information is not junk."

DMS kicked the entry into the garbage column on its maintenance report.

They had written a program to do the entry, so they ran the program a thousand times.

If DMS noticed, it didn't think anything of it. One thousand times it kicked the entry into the junk portion of the report.

"I don't think it knows what we're doing," Sydney said. "You know, analyzing reports may be unconscious."

"I don't think consciousness is an issue here," Damien said. "Remember the shark."

"Okay. Maybe it's involuntary. The shark has control over what fish it goes after, but it doesn't have control over its kidney function. It doesn't choose anything about kidney function. Maybe maintenance is involuntary."

Damien looked at her. She thought he was going to say something dismissive, but after a moment he said, "Well, then, what parts of it would be voluntary?"

Sydney shrugged. "I don't know. Epidemiologist, maybe. But we can't screw too much with that."

Screwing with maintenance was bad enough. But data from LEGBA went directly to the CDC and National Institute of Health through a weird subroutine called DAMBALLAH which did complicated pattern recognition and statistical stuff. Sydney worried about a couple of things. One was causing a system crash that meant someone ended up dying. The other was getting them in trouble with the CDC or the government. Of the two, she would have to choose getting in trouble, except she could imagine bad data to the CDC might mean someone ended up dying anyway. In her mind it unfolded: bad information seems to indicate a critical alert, Marburg virus reports in New York City seem to show that someone got off a plane and infected people with a hemorrhagic fever. The false epidemic pulls resources from a real outbreak of Legionnaires' disease, and people who would have lived now die because she and Damien were poking DMS.

She thought Damien would say to poke DAMBALLAH. Damien seemed a lot less concerned about getting in trouble than she did. She had a theory that the fear of getting in trouble was what made her not as good a programmer and that, in fact, it was all linked to testosterone, and that was why there were more guy programmers than women. It was a very hazy theory, and she didn't like it, but she had pretty much convinced herself it was true, although she couldn't bear to think of sharing it with anybody, because it was a lot better to think that there were social reasons why girls didn't usually become code monkeys than to think there were biological reasons. But right now she was pretty sure that she would say *stop* and Damien would say *go.*

He surprised her. "Not DAMBALLAH. You think that DMS might be fucking with the outputs on DAMBALLAH?"

She shrugged. "I don't know."

"Maybe tomorrow we can try to check that."

Tomorrow was tough, because when Sydney got home she was too keyed up to sleep, and she was up until almost four reading a book called *Dead Until Dark*. The book had been recommended to her by Addy, her college roommate from junior and senior years. It was the first in a series about a paranormal detective and had been just about the most perfect thing to read after coming home from a failed attempt to prove that a computer system was aware.

She was still worried about DAMBALLAH and whether DMS was doing weird things with the epidemiological reports. DAMBALLAH was a complicated system. It made decisions about reporting data. She couldn't easily check its decisions—that was the point. Every two weeks they got a report from the NIH and the CDC about epidemiological trends, and if there was something new that the CDC was looking for, say an outbreak of shigella in preschools in the South, there was an elaborate way they entered additional parameters to DAMBALLAH's tracking system. The CDC and the NIH also sent them error reports and WRs. WRs were to correct when DMS was reporting something that wasn't important or was overreporting. The result was the DMS "learned" epidemiology.

This made it difficult to know if DMS was screwing with the numbers. If DMS did report something, like an epidemic of onchocerciasis (parasitical river blindness) in Seattle, that would get caught fast. But if DMS were just, say, overreporting the incidence of TB in Seattle, that might not. Sydney ran an ep report and started working on a program that would check the DAMBALLAH database for raw numbers of cases of illnesses that DMS was tracking for the CDC, to see if she could spot anything that looked weird.

Damien had been cranky and quiet all day. Then at 3:17, the lights at Meridian Health in Macon, Georgia, did the wave. The same thing that had happened the day before happened again, except this time in reverse order, ending with DM Kensington Medical. They found out it was happening again when the power outage rolled through headquarters early in the sequence. Within minutes Tony, their boss, was screaming at people to stop it, but they decided that stopping it would be more complicated than letting it run its course, so they called the last three hospitals and gave them a heads-up.

Damien was set to write code that would catch the beginning of the sequence and stop it from happening. Together, he and Sydney pored over the tangle of spaghetti that was SAMEDI code. The next day, at 3:17 they could at least switch the electrical systems to maintenance mode for the time it took for DMS to run through its sequence. (According to the log, it would have started with DM Kensington again.) Hospitals bitched about slowdowns in the DMS while SAMEDI was not running. It shouldn't have affected everything else, but DMS was so weirdly interconnected that SAMEDI had evidently been doing something that optimized read/write functions. Which SAMEDI wasn't supposed to do at all.

"Why 3:17?" Sydney asked. "Why the electrical system?"

Damien shrugged. They were poring over printouts, looking for ways to, in Damien's words, "build a box around the bug." Tony was alternating between asking them if they'd found it yet and telling the head of operations that the admin IT team was doing a great job and to get out of their faces and let them work. Tony was a screamer, but as far as he was concerned, the only one allowed to scream at his people was him.

Mostly Sydney noticed that Damien did not seem to be "in the zone." He had talked a lot about being "in the zone." About time passing without his even realizing it. Pouing over printouts, he sighed, exasperated. He got up and went to the bathroom a lot. He got coffee a lot. He talked about what they might do, and although his ideas were smart, they more he talked the more she got an idea about how he thought about stuff like this; and for the first time she found herself thinking, maybe with some experience, she could code pretty good, too.

She finished her database checker for DAMBALLAH, the program that tracked disease trends. The results were mostly ... complicated. But there was one area she thought was a problem.

"Damien?" she said.

"Yeah?"

"I think DAMBALLAH is messing with the numbers."

He looked at her. Carefully he said, "How do you know?"

"I don't," she said. "Not for certain. But I ran a raw compilation of what was in the Seattle database, and compared it to what DMS is reporting. And DMS is reporting a nosocomial infection rate of seven percent." Benevola was involved in a big program to reduce nosocomial infections. Nosocomial infections were infections that the patient caught as a result of medical care. Benevola was working with a huge government double-blind study.

"And?" Damien said.

"I can only find evidence of less than a one percent nosocomial infection rate."

Tony, their boss, stood in his doorway. "What are you saying, Sydney?"

"I ... I'm not sure." Sydney wasn't ready to talk to Tony yet. Actually, Sydney was pretty much never ready to talk to Tony. But she had wanted to talk to Damien about this, first. "I mean, DAMBALLAH is cranking numbers in ways I don't understand. It could be that I don't recognize a lot of stuff that DAMBALLAH does. I mean, that's the whole point, right?"

Tony came by and leaned over the cube wall. "We might shut it down."

"Tonight?" Damien asked.

"No, shut it down and reload from a backup from twelve months ago." Tony always acted as if you were dim if you didn't get what he was talking about, but he had a tendency to start conversations somewhere in the middle, so everyone was always confused talking to him.

"We'll lose all our updates," Sydney said.

"Yeah," Tony said. "But if it's unstable, who cares? We'll look at reloading the system over the weekend. I gotta talk to upstairs first 'cause it will be a huge nightmare."

Understatement of the year.

When Tony had gone back in his office, Damien said, "Show me."

She showed him.

Damien nodded. "This is really smart. I mean, not the programming."

Sydney grinned, "A monkey could do the programming." It was an old joke.

"I wouldn't have thought to do this," Damien said.

"It might not mean anything," Sydney said. "I mean, the whole point is that DAMBALLAH is extrapolating information.

"It means we're killing DMS," Damien said.

"You said it wasn't alive," she said.

"Semantics," he said.

She went home and finished *Dead Until Dark*, started *Dark Hunter*, and fed Scott Pilgrim, her cat, and thought about DMS. What would it be like to be alone? Of course, as a human being, she was a social animal. Even the cat was a somewhat social animal. But DMS wasn't. DMS didn't even know anyone else existed. DMS lived in a data stream. In science fiction, AIs were always looking for other AIs or trying to be human, like Data on *Star Trek Next Gen.*

Truth was, she was beginning to get a feeling about DMS. About what DMS might be like. She felt as if she could sort of sense the edges of DMS's personality, and although she knew it wasn't true, she knew it was just because Damien had used it as an example, more and more she thought of DMS as a shark. Not in a predatory way. She had an image of a shark in her head, a small shark, a nurse shark. She could see its eye, a black circle in white, overly simple, like a ventriloquist's dummy. Although the whole point of DMS was that it was not someone else speaking through the code.

The shark in her head swam, purposeful and opaque, its eyes tracking, its mouth open and curved. Sharks don't have a neocortex. Their brain is simple. They aren't moral or immoral, ethical or unethical. DMS was like that, because for DMS, nothing else was alive. The world for DMS was data, and DMS swam in the data. She was beginning to feel as if she wanted it to. DMS was creepy.

She dragged herself in again the next day. She swore she would not read late. She would go to bed early.

The good news was, Damien was pretty sure they had a way to catch DMS when it started screwing with the electrical system. At 3:15, Tony and most of the department came over to watch. What Damien had done was make sure that when DMS did its electrical-system trick, the system would catch it as soon as the lights started going out and reroute so that DMS wasn't actually touching the electrical system. At 3:17, Damien and Sydney's printers started up. Damien had set them to send a report if DMS tried to do its thing.

DMS would know that the electrical system wasn't responding. Sydney imagined DMS trying to run the pattern that sent the black-out rolling and finding yet again that nothing was happening. Was it perplexing? If data was DMS's reality, and it couldn't affect the data, what would that mean for DMS?

She ran the program that sent DMS the string of a thousand 10101s, a thousand times.

Instantly, her printer light blinked. DMS had started the electrical pattern sequence again.

She ran the program again.

DMS started over again.

She ran the program a third time. And a third time her printer hummed. She ran the program a fourth time, thinking, "I'm talking to you. I'm responding to you. Do you know someone else is out here? Or is it like a toddler knocking something off a high chair just to see it fall?" The fourth time, there was no response. DMS didn't start the sequence that should have started the lights going out at DM Kensington Medical but which would, in actual fact, simply send an alert to Damien and Sydney. DMS had responded three times and ignored it the fourth. She felt a chill.

Years later, she would tell about this moment. There really wasn't enough proof to know that this wasn't just an intermittent software glitch. But she had believed at that moment that this was proof. DMS was choosing to act or not act. Software didn't choose. It ran. She would give talks and lectures and would come back to this moment again and again until like a coin it had worn so smooth that she couldn't actually feel anything about it. What should would never tell, and would eventually mostly forget, was how afraid she was.

"What the fuck are you doing?" Damien asked.

"It answered me," Sydney said. She told him.

"It doesn't mean anything," Damien said.

"What are you talking about?" Tony asked.

"Damien thinks that DMS might be aware," Sydney said.

"What the fuck?" Tony said. "I don't have time for this. Are you screwing around with this system? This four-point-two-million-dollar system on which people's lives depend?"

"I don't really think that," Damien said. "It was just kind of an idea to kick around, you know?" The look he shot Sydney was murderous.

"We're going to have to go to backup. This is a mess," Tony said. "Admin wants us to go back to when the system was stable. Damien, can you fly to Texas on Saturday?"

DMS wasn't "in one place." DMS was a complex system spread across multiple servers. Damien would end up spending the weekend in Texas, babysitting part of the reload.

Damien was looking at Sydney. She should have said, "We can't." She should have said, "It's aware. It's the only one of its kind." She should have said a lot of things. Instead she looked at her desk.

"Yeah," Damien said. "I can go. I'm racking up the comp time, Tony."

Tony waved his hand in a "don't talk about that now" way. "Sydney, can you write me a memo about the data corruption you're finding?"

"I don't know that it's really data corruption," Sydney said.

"I don't want to hear any more about this DMS-is-alive crap."

"I don't mean—DAMBALLAH might be catching things I'm not catching. The whole point is that DAMBALLAH is sorting the data."

"Yeah," Tony said, not really listening. "Write that up, too."

Somewhere, DMS sorted the data stream. She was pretty sure that the thing in the machine did not think someone was talking to it. Blind and deaf, DMS had tried to make something happen, and something else had happened. But ones and zeroes weren't interesting enough for DMS to keep doing it. There would be no Helen Keller–at-the-well moment for DMS. No moment when DMS felt something out there in the void, talking to it, when DMS knew it was not alone. Sharks do not worry about others. They don't care. DMS didn't care, wasn't alive. It was aware of something. Just not her.

Tony told them they would be working that weekend to do the reinstall from backup. Start figuring out what they needed to do.

It would be gone. No one would ever know that she had known, except Damien. Maybe. He certainly wasn't likely to say, "Hey, there was this AI and we killed it." No, he'd explain to her how it was never really alive, how it could be restarted, so it wasn't exactly dead.

DMS was not a shark. She didn't know what it was. Didn't know how to think about it. It was as opaque as a stone. Did it even care if it was or was not? It had no survival instinct.

They started figuring out what data they wanted to backup before the reinstall.

It was a dicey thing. People's lives couldn't be trusted to DMS. But DMS was aware. But DMS couldn't be downloaded to another machine and replaced with a back-up. DMS was a system, a bunch of programs and computers all tied together.

A couple of hours later, Sydney dug out the *Wired* magazine with the interview with the guy from MIT who thought some systems had become aware. She sat at her desk for a while. Then she called MIT. "I'd like to talk to Professor Ayrton Tavares, please."

She was forwarded. "This is Kaleisha," a voice said.

"Can I talk to Professor Tavares?" Sydney asked.

"He's not available right now," the woman said. "Can I take a message?"

Sydney thought about saying, "no." She was going to get in trouble for this. Benevola. They weren't in the business of protecting nascent AIs. They were supposed to manage hospitals. "I'm a computer tech working on a big system like the ones that Professor Tavares talked about in the *Wired* article."

"Yes?" said the woman.

"I'm pretty sure I've got proof that our system is aware. Like the ones in the article. And they're going to shut it down."

In the end, they would shut the system down. Benevola would fire Sydney for divulging proprietary information. She would go to grad school for urban planning.

But at that moment, she hung up the phone and went to find Damien. DMS was still swimming in the data stream. The future was still probabilities, not actualities.

"Damien," she said, "I called Ayrton Tavares."

Damien said, "Who?" Not really paying attention. The name meant nothing to him.

"The AI guy. The one in the *Wired* article."

The look Damien gave her was naked and exposed. Too late she remembered that she wasn't supposed to know that Damien had found the article in *Wired*. Too late she realized that her whole relationship with Damien rested on the understanding that he was the guru, the smart one. He was Obi Wan. She was just a girl whom he could explain things to. She had known it all along, at some level, but this was the first time she'd forgotten to uphold her end of the bargain.

Maybe she thought for a moment that like DMS, she didn't care. But of course, she did.

Four years later, Rochester Institute of Technology would build a system that simulated DMS's environment and load DMS. Despite the differences between the original hardware and RIT's simulation, DMS would come back as if no time had passed at all. At 3:17, DMS would try to run the lights.

Going to France

In the beginning, there were only the three of them, and I had
met them quite by accident. The man sitting in the prow of the
skiff was a short, brown-haired Englishman. He was smiling in a
self-deprecating way. He was hunched forward, and he looked a little
gray. I thought he was scared but trying not to make a big deal out
of it. I gathered he had been sick, although he didn't say so directly.
He looked a little like a refugee, I thought. It was some sort of thing
about his heart, maybe? Not a heart attack, but perhaps angina. I was
worried for him, and so was the red-haired woman he was with.

"You need to eat," the red-haired woman said. "Have another
one of the granola bars." She was direct and not sentimental. She
didn't fuss. They didn't talk much.

"How long have you lived in the States?" I asked the Englishman.

"Eighteen years," he said. "My family says I sound like an
American."

He didn't. He had a neat little Van Dyke beard. He worked in
California, doing something in the television industry. One of those
mysterious credits at the end, AGD Assistant. Best Boy.

The breeze plucked at his shirt, a cotton, short-sleeved thing,
faded-looking but clean. Where had they done laundry?

The red-haired woman had a kind of crisp confidence about
her. She wasn't British. She was a paralegal from California. The third
woman they had just found traveling through Nevada. I steered the

boat out into the Atlantic. The sea was just a little choppy and gray, a very Atlantic early morning, I thought.

There was something wrong with the third woman. She was young, maybe twenty? She was short, and she looked wrong. Not Down syndrome, maybe autistic? She never spoke. The other two included her without particularly looking at or speaking to her. It was just that they all had this thing in common, that they could fly. They had come east across the U.S., flying by day, like hitchhikers or something, only not needing rides. They were going to fly to France. Since they couldn't actually fly when they were sleeping, this was dangerous, and yet they felt they had to. They didn't talk about it. But the Englishman was the most worried. He had been brushed by mortality, and the crisp woman seemed caught up in dealing with logistics, and the autistic one was just pure compulsion.

The little outboard motor puttered. I asked the Englishman if he had been to Paris. "Years ago," he said. "Back in the seventies. When I was a student, before I came to the States. Disco and all that."

I wondered why they could fly. I wished I could fly. I had had flying dreams. I had met them coming down the street in the early early morning, and the crisp woman had asked me if I knew someone who could take them out to sea. They were empty-handed, except that the crisp woman had a fanny pack. The autistic one was wearing a long red dress, burgundy really, the hem dirty. She had those soft, naturally red lips that some children have. The kind that make me feel that perhaps there is too much saliva involved.

I asked them why they needed to go out to sea, and the crisp woman said they needed a head start on their crossing. They didn't hide that they could fly. I thought they were tired of hiding and traveling to get to the ocean and now that it was so near, they were just shedding things, becoming their own essential selves and their compulsion. They showed me how they flew, the woman leaning her head back and spreading her arms a little away from her sides and then just rising. She went up about five feet and then dropped back down to land on the sidewalk, next to the neighbor's wall which was covered with bougainvillea, now bright red in the pale and slanted morning light.

"How are you going to cross the Atlantic?" I asked.

They just shrugged. "We don't know," the Englishman admitted.

What was I going to do, call the police? So I walked down to the beach with them, and then they climbed into my little aluminum skiff, the Englishman sitting slightly hunched in the prow. I gave him an aspirin and a granola bar and gave the other two granola bars, too. They were nice, in a distracted sort of way. I felt as if I was smuggling refugees, maybe off a Caribbean island in the dawn of an insurrection, a bloody revolution that would rise up against anyone perceived as a colonial. It was a funny little fantasy.

When we had gone out about a mile I saw some other boats, clustering. The Englishman, the crisp woman, and I saw them, and we headed for them. They bobbed a bit, clustered together, all different kinds of boats but most of them bigger than mine. It turned out that there were about eighteen of the flyers, all drawn to the Atlantic and needing to fly to France. I recognized one of them—my high school American Literature teacher, a small and very quiet woman who looked, appropriately enough, a little like Emily Dickinson and whom I hadn't seen in over ten years. She was wearing a cardigan sweater and white pants and looked birdlike. She smiled at me, but in a kind of courteous way. I didn't think she recognized me. I had changed since then. A lot more than she had.

The crisp woman cupped her hands and hulloed.

A man from one of the other boats called back, "We're going to follow a cruise ship, so we have some place at night."

There was a general brightening up of the three of us, excluding, of course, the autistic woman, who was looking at the other boats and humming. The Englishman still looked rueful.

"Maybe you could go without flying yourself?" I asked. But he only shook his head.

By then the sun was well up and the haze had burned off and they all stood up and sort of let their shoulders go back and drop. Their chests rising and opening in a way that would please my yoga teacher, they began one by one to rise.

Once back on land, I realized that I could go to France, too. I couldn't fly, but I could fly in an airplane. I went straight home and got on Priceline and, without telling anyone, booked a ticket to Paris that afternoon. It only cost about two thousand dollars. I put in that I would come back at the end of the month, although I didn't really know. I was delighted that I could actually get a ticket right then and there, for that day. It was like something in a movie.

And good thing I had. I went straight to the airport even though my plane wouldn't leave until nine that evening. Like the fliers, I didn't take much. I went dressed in my old T-shirt and exercise pants, but I did have to take a little bag with my wallet and my passport. When I got to the airport there were dozens of people who had dropped everything to go to France. Most of them were having trouble getting tickets, and some of them were making elaborate arrangements that would take them to Germany or Ireland or even to Italy before they could get to France. I had been lucky that my compulsion was not so strong that I couldn't stop and get on Priceline.

I went to the gate, which was in a special part of the airport for Internationals, where the floor wasn't carpet, just tile. The Duty Free shop was open. Such a nice phrase, "Duty Free." Actually, I kind of like having a duty, though. In the end, I couldn't go empty-handed the way the fliers had. I had packed a shirt, a pair of jeans, and underwear in a little bag I used for yoga. I had packed a towel, too, because it was always in the bag anyway, along with my shampoo and deodorant in case I had to meet a client after yoga class.

A guy named Brian who had a boat and who had been out on the water that morning with the fliers said that going to Ireland wouldn't be so bad. It was at least on the way. Lindbergh had stopped at Ireland on his way to France, hadn't he?

I didn't think he had, but one of the reasons I had started taking yoga was to be less self-centered which in my case meant less of a know-it-all and even though most of the time I still corrected people and pontificated and even in yoga class still wanted the teacher to notice how good I was doing, I didn't say anything this time.

Brian didn't have any luggage or any carry-on, which had caused him a lot of trouble at the airport, because not having luggage is a sign that you might be a terrorist. I'd had to surrender my deodorant and shampoo because they were more than three ounces. But Brian had been searched and interviewed. There were so many people there who wanted to go to France that someone finally realized that it was not a plot but something else. Brian said one of the TSA guys was trying to go to France and he explained it, although how it could be explained I don't know.

I'm sure there were people there who were flying to France for other reasons, like vacations or work, but those of us who were just Going to France seemed to be most of the passengers. We sat around without the usual airport feeling, because it didn't matter what time we left or got there, about luggage and reservations or connections or schedules. It's amazing how nice an airport is when you're not worried.

It's true that we are free to do whatever we want, even go to France on a whim. We can make any choice we want. We can do anything we want. We just have to not care about consequences.

I didn't care about consequences, but at about seven, I knew I wasn't going to France. I didn't say anything to anyone, not even Brian, who I knew was going. I could tell that several other people weren't going. We just weren't. We didn't have the Going to France look any-more. I stopped at the ticket counter on my way out and explained to them that I wasn't going and that I didn't have any luggage so they wouldn't think since I didn't get on the plane that there was some ter-rorist threat. I didn't want the people like Brian to be delayed. I can-celed my ticket, even though it was nonrefundable. Maybe someone else could go. I got in my car and went home.

It wasn't that I couldn't go to France, it was just that I wasn't. Maybe it had worn off. Maybe I had caught a mild case from the fliers, but it hadn't lasted. I didn't know. I felt kind of sad. When I got home, I didn't want to go in my house.

I left my bag in my car and started walking to my mother's house. My mother lived in the same house she had since I was ten, a little brick ranch. It was a couple of miles away and I had never walked there before because I had to cross several major streets. But that night, I walked. My neighborhood is full of old split-levels and even smaller houses, like mine, which only has two bedrooms and no basement. As I walked farther, I went through a neighborhood full of newer, bigger, two-story homes. One of the houses, which was brick on the bottom half and siding on the top, now had a huge clock in the side of it. The clock was set in a huge wave of metal, shining pink in the setting sun. I went this way to the grocery, and the house had never had a clock in it before. It was big, with an ornate hour and minute hand and no numbers, just an ivory face with a design like ivy down near where the seven would have been. But the siding around the clock had been changed into some substance like porcelain that rose and swirled, organic. Suburbia has always struck me as a little strange, but before it had been a boring, overly sincere falseness, and it was as if that clock was about a different suburbia full of beautiful manmade things, full of artifice.

I thought about my mother's house, walking through the dark-ness. When I got there, it would be the end of the day and maybe I'd have a daiquiri or a Manhattan, and maybe my mother would have one with me. I didn't really know if I wanted a drink, but it was a kind of punctuation on the day.

I was at an intersection; traffic lights, four lanes wide plus turn lanes in all directions, waiting to cross, maybe only half a mile from my mother's house. A dry cleaner, a drug store, buildings all pressed close to the street without much space between them. A Ford pickup was stopped at the light in one direction. The sky was dark but still glowed purple and luminous the way it will some nights, especially before a tornado. A young unkempt guy with a beard sprinted across the light, and an SUV coming around the corner fast lost it trying to avoid him and went up on two wheels as it started to roll over and everything froze in place. I could see the underside of the SUV, all that car stuff of struts and differentials and muffler and catalytic converter. I looked around. Time wasn't stopped. The DON'T WALK light was flashing, and although things were frozen, it was imperfect, and after a moment, like the moment of a held breath, the truck floored it and went through the intersection past the frozen tumbling SUV. The guy running had only one foot on the ground, but his raised left foot wiggled back and forth on his ankle, as if he was finding his way to movement. A big orange sneaker, with a big white toe, waggling.

I looked at it all and I knew it was all right. It was only just beginning.

Honeymoon

I was an aggravated bride. It was a little after one in the morning, I guess. We were supposed to be on our way to the Hampton Inn in Columbus for our wedding night. I was aggravated a lot with Chris, but never this aggravated before. I was walking back toward Lancaster on Route 33, glad that for the reception I had changed into a pair of white canvas sneakers with sequins that my cousin Linda had decorated for the wedding. I knew that I wouldn't want to wear heels all night. I'm a big girl, and I wasn't going to miss dancing at my own reception because my feet hurt too bad. But I was still wearing my wedding dress and my veil.

Chris was in his F-150 pickup, driving slow so he could keep asking me to get in the truck. You wouldn't think there were that many cars on Route 33 at that time of the morning, but there were, and they kept slowing down and carefully passing. Some guy called out the window, "I'll give you a ride, honey!"

I gave him the finger.

"Please, please get in the truck, Kayla," Chris said.

I wasn't talking to him. Usually when I got angry, I started crying, which always loses you any sort of chance you have of making a point. But I was so mad that night, I never even shed a tear.

"I'm sorry. Baby, I'm sorry, I'll make it up to you," Chris said.

I couldn't stand that. "Just how are you going to make it up to me?" I said. "How are you going to give me back my wedding night?"

He looked at me with big puppy eyes and said, "Don't be like that, Kayla."

It had been a really nice wedding. I saved the money. My dad's on disability, so I wasn't going to ask him for it. I'm an assistant manager at McDonald's, and I'd taken a second job working for Allwood Florists. All last fall I had made Christmas ornaments—wooden soldiers and Santas and reindeer. I sold them at craft shows. The biggest sellers were dog bone ornaments that I would personalize with the dog's name. I worked my butt off. Marty at Allwood gave me an employee rate for my wedding flowers; red roses and lilies. I got my dress in Pennsylvania, because if you're from out of state you don't have to pay sales tax. I spent a hundred and forty dollars on my hair, having it highlighted. I went to the tanning salon—my dress showed off my shoulders, which are one of my best features. I really did look the best I have ever looked. And the reception went pretty good. A lot of people didn't stay, but a few people stayed until midnight.

I was really proud of the job I did. Chris had gotten a roofing job for his neighbor in June and said he would put the seven hundred dollars he earned toward our honeymoon. He wanted to take care of it. I gave him the money I had and he said he'd taken care of it. We were going to Cancun even though everyone said it was too hot in August. But I'd never been to another country. So we were supposed to go to Columbus, spend the night, and then catch our flight in the morning.

Except that while we were on our way to Columbus, Chris told me that he hadn't actually taken care of it.

"Don't be mad, Kayla," he said. "Listen to me first."

He and Felter and Carnegie had gone up to Windsor in June, right after the roofing job. I knew that. I figured that after we got married he wouldn't be able to hang out with his friends as much and besides, I was working all the time anyway, paying for the wedding. They were playing blackjack and he won a bunch a money. "Almost six hundred dollars!" he said. "I was gonna use it on our honeymoon. I thought I was on a roll, you know?"

Chris was looking at me. He has really cute blue eyes. Usually I can't believe that a heavy girl like me got someone like Chris.

"So what happened," I asked.

"I don't know," he said. "I mean, I know, but you know, I can't explain it. I wanted to win big. I wanted to get the honeymoon suite, you know? You worked so hard—"

"What happened?" I said.

"I lost the money," he said. "I'm sorry."

No honeymoon. He was hoping to put the Hampton Inn on his credit card, but he didn't know if he'd be able to, because it was kind of close to maxed out. He'd meant to get it paid down, maybe put the whole honeymoon on it, but the alternator went on the truck, and he needed it to get to work.

"Why didn't you tell me?" I said. I didn't know what else to say. I didn't really believe him. I just couldn't think about it. It kept squirming around in my head like I understood it, but I didn't at the same time.

"I didn't want to ruin the wedding," he said.

I had worked really hard on the wedding, but I guess I hadn't thought a whole lot about Chris. I was looking at him, and it occurred to me that the reason Chris was with a girl like me was because he was a fuck-up. I'd just never admitted it to myself.

"Stop the truck," I said.

I knew I couldn't walk all the way back to Lancaster, so I finally called Sarah, my best friend and maid of honor. Then I sat down on the berm and waited. Chris pulled the truck off the road and stood, looking awkward. He started to sit down next to me, but I said, "Don't sit down. That tux is rented and I'm not paying extra if you get it dirty."

While I was waiting for her, I told Chris I was going to get the marriage annulled.

"What does that mean?" he asked.

"It's like a divorce, only it's like the wedding never happened," I said.

"But it did happen," he said.

"It was never consummated," I said. I don't even know where I had heard about that.

He didn't understand what I meant by that, either.

"We didn't have sex on our wedding night," I said.

"We've been having sex for two years," he said.

We had, ever since I was seventeen and in my junior year at high school and he was thinking he would go into the army when he graduated. I figured if I had sex with him, he'd stay. "But we didn't do it tonight," I said. "So it doesn't count."

I moved to Cleveland, because my cousin Donna lives there. Donna is the opposite of me, physically. She's short and skinny and has dark brown hair. She has the family boobs, though. She weighs 105 pounds and the joke is that fifty pounds of it is in her chest. She's in nursing school, and she said I could get a job at the hospital. I never wanted to be a nurse, but she said there were lots of jobs in a hospital, and I could stay with her. I got a job in the kitchen which was fine. The hospital is the Cleveland Clinic, which is probably the world's biggest hospital. It's a lot bigger than Lancaster. Not in square miles, but I'd bet more people work at Cleveland Clinic than live in Lancaster, Ohio. It's really modern. Lots of buildings with green glass. Rich foreigners like Sheiks come there when they're sick. The kitchens have to make all sorts of food. Diabetic food, low-protein food, low-fat food, Muslim food, Jewish food. It was a lot more interesting than McDonald's.

I'd never worked with so many black people before. There are black people in Lancaster, but not so many of them. The black people at the Cleveland Clinic, a lot of them were real ghetto. Sometimes if they were talking to each other I couldn't understand what they were saying. I'd always liked country, for one thing. I didn't like hip-hop.

Donna was great about me living there, but it was a pain. I thought about going back to Lancaster. In a lot of ways, living in Cleveland wasn't a whole lot different than living in Lancaster, except it took a lot longer to get to work. My marriage had been annulled. It turned out sex didn't have anything to do with it.

Chris kept calling me and asking me to come home. I asked if he could take me out on a date. He showed up at Donna's with a dozen roses and got down on one knee. Then he called collect when he was drunk and cried.

I was talking to my dad one night—I called him every Tuesday—and complaining about Chris, and my dad said, "Well, Kayla, what did you expect?"

"I expect him to act like a man," I said.

My dad chuckled and I knew he was thinking that was too much to expect of Chris. It occurred to me that maybe my dad had figured out what Chris was like a long time ago. "Do you like Chris?" I asked.

"It doesn't matter now, does it?" my dad said. I could just picture him, sitting in the recliner. My dad lives in Chauncy. He used to work for Diamond, before they closed the mill, then he worked at Lancaster Correctional. So I grew up in Lancaster. But when he had to stop working on account of his back, he moved back to Chauncy with my grandmother. Chauncy is about the size of one floor of one build-ing of the Cleveland Clinic. When he said that, I knew he hadn't ever really thought much of Chris. Although he was always nice enough to him, and they joked around.

"Why didn't you tell me?" I asked.

He sighed. I thought he was going to say that he didn't want to interfere. "I thought you wanted to wear the pants," he said.

I've always wanted a strong man. Or I thought I did. Maybe I thought a pickup truck and talking about the army meant Chris was a strong guy. Or maybe my dad was right. Maybe I wanted to wear the pants.

Maybe I hadn't really been fair to Chris. But when he called, I would say to myself, Be fair, Kayla. And the sound of his voice would make this feeling rise up in me, like the feeling of teeth scraping together, or like the weird rubbing noise that my car was making. Kind of a clicking noise. It was kind of hard to hear, and so I found myself listening to it and getting more and more tense as I drove to work. That was what talking to Chris was like. I got tenser and tenser while he talked.

My car was sounding like my relationship with Chris, so of course, one day it stopped working altogether. It was the timing belt. It cost me seventy-four dollars to get it towed. Then they told me that it would cost over six hundred to get it fixed, and that I was lucky I was on Euclid and not the highway because if it had been on the highway it might have thrown a rod, and then I might as well just get a new car.

I don't even know what "throwing a rod" is, but I sort of picture pieces of metal flying through the hood or something. The next time Chris called I told him about it, and for the first time in a long time he perked up. "Yeah, yeah, you could have been in big trouble."

"I am in big trouble," I said. "I'm taking the bus to work. The bus is creepy, and it takes forever. It's going to cost six hundred dollars to get it fixed." I was trying to save money to get a place of my own and let poor Donna have her apartment back. But I didn't have six hundred dollars and I was going to have to put it on my credit card. My credit card still had stuff on it from the wedding. Donna was paying for nursing school and only working two days a week at the hospital.

"So are you going to come home?" he asked.

"I'd rather die," I said.

Donna's dad, my Uncle Jim, loaned me the money to get my car fixed, and I promised to pay him back, a hundred dollars a month.

One of the girls in the kitchen told me about medical studies. How she got paid a hundred dollars to take cough medicine every day for two weeks. She told me where to check out the list of studies, and during my dinner break I went about six blocks to the building where she told me. I got lost once—I know how to get to where I park and then to where I work, but the rest of the place is still a maze.

There was a list of stuff, but nothing like the cough medicine study. It was all weird stuff—studies on depression, on taking estrogen. I looked over the whole list and couldn't find a thing I could qualify for. While I was looking, a guy came up to look, too. He looked healthy. He was a couple of years older than me. Short. Built like he wrestled, if you know what I mean.

He wrote down the info on the psoriasis study.

"What is that?" I asked.

"It's a skin problem," he said. "Your skin gets dry and flaky."

That sounded vaguely possible, although mostly my skin is too oily. "My feet get that way," I said. "Would that be enough?"

"To be psoriasis?" he said. "Probably not. But you don't have to have psoriasis to be in the study. They need healthy people for comparison. Tell Lisa you want on the list."

I did. She asked me about my psoriasis and I told her I didn't have it. She nodded and put me down. Two weeks later I got called to be in the control group.

And that was my first medical study.

Psoriasis studies are pretty good. I got one hundred and fifty dollars to put cream on and be examined once a week for twelve weeks. Fifty dollars a month toward what I owed Uncle Jim helped a lot.

I got a job in a catering hall as a cook and left the Clinic, but I kept doing medical studies. A study on asthma got me enough to cover the deposit on an apartment. Which was good, because Donna had met Ted, and they were talking marriage, and they sure didn't need me around the apartment. She graduated from nursing school and one November day, as I walked from the parking garage at the Clinic, I realized that I had lived in Cleveland for three years. The wind cut between the buildings the way it always does. The streets were a mess of slush. I was looking for a study so I could save money for a trip to Cancun in February.

The idea for the trip had started in the fall, when I called Sarah, who had been my maid of honor, and she told me Chris was getting married again. I knew I shouldn't care, but I wasn't even seeing a guy. Not that I wanted Chris. And I had a great life. Good friends. Four of us were going—two girls I worked with and another friend I had met at Weight Watchers. Weight Watchers hadn't been much of a success for me or for Melinda, but we started going out to movies and hanging out. We call ourselves the Fat Fab Four. Mel started it, and she really is Fab. She wears jeans and skirts, and I can remember her taking off like four hundred silver bracelets to get weighed. I love her style. Everybody had heard the story of how I didn't get to go to Cancun on my honeymoon. Mel had a friend who was a travel agent, and she got us a great deal—seven days, all inclusive, for fourteen hundred dollars apiece. So it was the Fat Fab Four Not-A-Honeymoon Vacation.

Lisa was still working the desk. She said, "Hi, Kayla, I haven't seen you for a while." I hadn't done a study for ages. I could still use the money, but I'd been busy with the FF4.

I studied the list, but nothing looked good. Some things I just won't do. Anything that looks like it will hurt. I did a burn cream study once where they actually gave me a little burn on my butt. Hurt like hell. So now I'm more careful.

I was frowning.

Lisa said, "What about the pulmonary study?"

I shook my head. "I'm going out of town." The pulmonary study required that I be available for four months. The whole point of doing a study was to help pay for Cancun, not cancel it.

"This just came in," Lisa said. "Have you ever done a Phase I drug trial?"

I had done some drug trials, but they were all for stuff like psoriasis and the burn study. This paid two thousand dollars. It was for a leukemia drug. I'd never done something where you had to take a serious drug. But two thousand dollars was a lot. The whole trip, and spending money. They only wanted twelve people.

She handed me the fact sheet. It had all the usual warnings. This drug is untested on humans ... risk ...

Normally I wouldn't have done anything like this. But the chance to make two thousand dollars seemed too good to pass up. Like it was almost fate, you know? I don't know that I believe in fate, especially now, but it seemed that way at the time. So I signed up.

The trial was on a Thursday afternoon. To get the day off I had to swap with someone else, which meant working a double on Saturday—wedding in the morning, and another wedding in the evening. At least in the evening I'd be doing bar, which wasn't so bad. Handing out glasses of wine and beer to happy drunken wedding guests.

Thursday I went to a medical lab out on Cedar Road.

The Cleveland Clinic has three zones, and it's all about patients. The front zone where the patients first see the hospital—the lobbies and the doctors' offices—is really nice. Nice carpeting, nice wood, nice chairs and tables. Plants. Artwork. Then there's the middle zone, places like the surgical staging areas and the hospital rooms. The hospital rooms try to be nice, but they have to have all this equipment and it's not like television. It's kind of cluttered and busy, and there will be stacks of blankets, boxes of latex gloves. Everything feels a little crowded. There's no art on the walls of the ER or the outpatient staging and recovery areas.

Then there's the back zone. Maintenance and the kitchen, offices and the places where the actual technicians do the lab work. Basements and closets. Hard light or not enough light. Notices and memos stuck on the wall. "Employees Must Wash Hands Before Returning to Work"; "Mandatory Meeting on Health Coverage Changes"; Waste Stock tracking sheets. That was the kind of place where the drug trial took place.

It was a pretty large room with no windows and a linoleum floor. It had one of those long folding tables like you see in a school cafeteria. On the table were vials and cotton swabs, syringes and gloves. A nurse was sitting in a folding chair reading a paperback.

There were ten of us, all guys except for me and one other woman. A lab tech checked us off on a clipboard, and we all had a packet sitting on a plastic chair. "Please sit in the chair with your packet," the guy with the clipboard said. "The dosages have been calculated based on your weight, and if you sit in someone else's chair, that could compromise the study." Then he came to each of us and asked us our name and our birthdate and gave us each a hospital bracelet with all that and an ID number on it. He explained how we would be asked the same thing again before receiving the injection, and that was just to make sure that there were no slip-ups.

Then he explained about double-blind trials. No one in this room, he explained, knew which of us were getting the drug for testing and which were getting the placebo, which was just an injection of saline. He explained phase one testing. The point of this test, he explained, was not to determine if the drug worked, but just to confirm that it was safe for people. This drug, the one we were getting, had been extensively tested on rabbits and monkeys. Rabbits and monkeys, of course, could not report adverse affects, so we were to report any adverse affects we experienced. We would be getting a much smaller dose than the rabbits and monkeys.

I was the second person in the line of chairs. The guy sitting next to me was wearing a plaid shirt and thermal undershirt and work boots. He looked like he did construction. "Have you ever done this before?" I asked.

He nodded. "I've done two others, but they didn't pay as good as this."

A nurse came and asked him his name, date of birth, and ID number. She took a blood sample from him and then wrote his ID number on a label and stuck it on. Then she did the same thing to me.

As she moved down the chairs, I looked in my packet. The drug we were taking didn't have a real name. It was just called GNT1146. It was for leukemia, lupus, and MS. Which, I will tell you, made me feel a little glad. It's hard to think you're doing much for humanity when you're getting paid to not have psoriasis in a psoriasis study. But what if this drug really cured people with MS? I said that to the guy in the flannel shirt.

He kind of looked at me. He made me think a little of Chris, I don't know why. Maybe because he was wearing a Ford cap.

"Is that why you're doing this?" he asked me.

"Hell no," I said. "I need the money to go to Cancun."

That made him grin. "Yeah, that sounds good," he said. He didn't know what he was going to do with the money. He's heard about it from his cousin's girlfriend, who worked somewhere doing some kind of paperwork for medical stuff. He figured he should pay down his credit card, but he was also thinking of saving it toward a down payment on a motorcycle.

The guy with the clipboard started talking, so we shut up, although all he did was tell us the same thing that was in the packet and make us all sign that we understood the risks. It was just like school. I underlined *Phase 1 Drug Trial: Ten to twenty healthy adults.* Phase two is something like fifty sick people. If the stuff doesn't seem to be as good as what people get anyway, then they stop. Otherwise they go to phase three. (I wondered what it would be like to have leukemia and find out that the experimental drug you are taking didn't do as good as what normal people get. I decided I was probably not brave enough for phase two, if I ever got leukemia.) Phase three has a couple of thousand sick people in it. Most drugs never get beyond phase two, the guy with the clipboard explained.

About that time, I admit, I zoned out. One of the fluorescents was in the flicker-before-dying stage, and it was annoying me. We had been there over an hour before the nurse finally started giving us injections.

The guy in the flannel shirt took off his shirt and rolled up his thermal undershirt. Then the nurse wrote down the time and his ID number. She asked me my name and birthdate and ID number but didn't give me the shot. I asked why.

"We wait two minutes between injections," she said.

"Watching for green and purple spots?" said the guy putting back on his flannel shirt.

"Purple and pink," she said.

We all three grinned.

Finally, I got my shot.

Then I had to sit there while they gave the next eight people the shot, wondering if my growing headache was a drug effect or the result of the bad fluorescent light. After the last person had gotten the shot, I thought we would maybe fill out some more paperwork and be told when to come back for follow-up. But we still sat there. I figured we'd been told how long we would sit there some time after I stopped paying attention. I was embarrassed to admit I had, so I sat there, thinking about where I was going to eat when I left.

I finally decided I could ask Mr. Green and Purple Spots. I started to say something just as he said, "I don't feel so good."

"What's wrong?" I asked.

"I feel sick," he said. "Like I've got a fever." He was shaking.

"Hey," I said, to get the nurse's attention. "This guy doesn't feel good."

He took off his flannel shirt. "I'm burning up," he said, and rubbed his head, hard.

She came over and asked him to describe how he felt.

"Is this an adverse effect?" he asked.

"I don't know," she said.

Just our luck, I thought. We get a nurse who doesn't know what she's doing. But now I wonder if they weren't allowed to say anything. Or probably she really didn't know if he just happened to be sick or not.

"Can I have an aspirin or something?" he asked.

"Let's wait a bit," she said.

I didn't know what to do. Everyone else was leaning forward, looking at us. Looking at the sick guy.

"What's wrong with him?" someone asked the clipboard guy.

"I don't know," the clipboard guy said.

After a few minutes, the guy on the other side of me said, "I feel sick."

The nurse came over and laid her hand against his forehead. I was surprised she didn't have one of those temperature thingies that they stick in your ear. This guy was shaking, too. "I'm gonna be sick," he said. The nurse ran and grabbed the trash can and he vomited into it.

My stomach rose, and I looked away. I thought maybe we weren't supposed to leave our seats, but when the flannel shirt guy threw up, I got up and walked over to the wall.

"Are you all right?" the clipboard guy asked me.

"I think so," I said, although I didn't know.

Then the fourth person started throwing up.

"God," said the first guy. "My head feels like it's exploding!"

Everybody who wasn't throwing up was looking at me, or looking at the fifth person, who was the other woman. She was a black woman, maybe in her thirties? She looked scared.

"Can I have something for the pain, please!" said the first guy.

The third guy was lying on the floor now, and the nurse was kneeling next to him. "He's dizzy," she said. "I think from spiking a fever." She pointed to the table where the cotton swabs and stuff were and said to the guy with the clipboard, "There's packets of Tylenol over there, give him one."

Clipboard guy said to her, "Should I call EMTs?"

"I don't know," she said. "This is your protocol."

"She's not sick," he pointed to the black woman.

"She might be a placebo," the nurse said. "How many placebos are there?"

"I don't know," he said.

"God!" said the first guy. "Of, God, please! My head!"

The nurse got him a Tylenol, which by this time seemed a little like pouring a glass of water on a house fire.

"I want to go home," the first guy said. "Call my girlfriend. I don't care about the money, I just want to go home."

"You stay here," the nurse said. "You're better here than home."

The clipboard guy was on his cell phone to someone. "I think you better send a doctor," I heard him say, and then he saw me watching him and turned his back to us so he was facing the wall.

The black woman didn't get sick. The guy next to her didn't get sick, either. And then the guy next to him seemed okay, although I hadn't been watching the time, so I didn't know how long it had been. Time was going so slow.

Then that next guy said, "Oh, man, I feel it."

It was like that story in the Bible, where the Israelites want to leave Egypt and they smear blood on their doors and God sends the angel of death to slay all the firstborn but passes over the houses marked with lamb's blood. Except we didn't know who had been marked and who had been saved.

A doctor showed up in about half an hour, but by that time they had called EMTs. Six people had gotten the drug and four were placebos, and we placebos were all standing around not looking at each other or looking at the sick guys. They loaded the sick ones into ambulances. The nurse was standing there in the hallway, holding her fist to her mouth like she was trying not to cry. I wanted to ask her if anything had ever happened like this before, but it was pretty clear no one had a clue.

I drove home.

I stopped on the way home and got a hamburger, but it seemed strange to eat it. I felt like I should be so upset I couldn't eat. Like that ever happened. When I got home I thought to check my cell phone— I had turned it off when I got to the medical trial because at Cleveland Clinic we weren't supposed to have our cell phones on inside the building. There was a message from a representative of the company that was doing the study, asking me to call. I called my friend Mel instead and told her what had happened, and she said she'd come over as soon as she got off work.

The phone rang as soon as I hung up, and it was NewsChannel5. I told them I didn't know if I was allowed to talk, but when they asked me if I could confirm that six people had gotten sick, I said that was true. Then the newspaper called. My cell kept ringing and ringing, until finally I shut it off and turned on the TV.

Mel got there just about the time that it came on the news, so I almost missed the first part. Not that it was very exciting. This news woman with really stiff, unmoving newscaster hair said that six people went to the hospital in a drug trial that had gone horribly wrong. The six men were hospitalized in critical condition with multiple organ failures. Then they showed the outside of a hospital—not Cleveland Clinic, maybe University Hospital?

"Fuck," Mel said, "that's so stupid."

I didn't know what she meant.

"Showing the outside of the hospital. It's just a building."

I said, "It's where they are."

"So?" she said. "What does showing you the hospital tell you? It's like when they are talking about a car accident and they show you this perfectly normal stretch of road with cars whizzing by."

Mel was really mad. It seemed a weird thing to be mad about.

"It's wrong," she said. When she lifted her hands, her bangles jingled. "It makes everything seem normal."

"They have to show something," I said, although that sounded lame.

"No they don't," she said. "We could go back to Miss My-Hair-Wouldn't-Move-in-a-Hurricane." She shook her head. "I don't know. Are you okay?"

"Yeah," I said. "Nothing happened to me."

"I don't know why it pisses me off so much," she said. "It's just the news."

The next day they had an interview with the girlfriend of one of the guys who got sick. She said that her boyfriend was in a coma and his head had swelled up to three times its normal size and he looked like the Elephant Man. I didn't think she should have said that. She should have given him his dignity. All day at work I told people what had happened. People wanted to know if I was going to sue. For what? They had told us that there was a risk. They've got to test drugs, or people would still be dying of plague and polio. It wasn't anybody's fault. It was just something that happened. I explained it over and over again. But people kept saying to me, "Are you going to sue?"

On Saturday I was so tired of the whole thing, I didn't want to talk about it anymore.

I wished I could find out what happened to the construction guy, the guy in the flannel shirt. Four of the guys were out of ICU in a couple of days, and I hoped he was one of them. I hoped he wasn't the guy whose girlfriend had said his head swelled up.

Then the news stopped talking about it.

It was almost like it had never happened. I got a check from the company that did the drug trial, and I put it in my bank account. It was weird because in some ways it was a bigger deal when Chris and I got our marriage annulled. People talked about that for a long time, and not just in Lancaster. But even Mel didn't talk to me about the drug trial thing unless I brought it up.

It didn't bother me, not really. I think about it sometimes. I'm not doing any more medical trials. I figure I gave my all for science already. But other than that, it's just something that happened.

We went to Cancun, my Not-A-Honeymoon-Trip to Cancun. We stayed in a resort hotel with a pool that went halfway around the hotel and had two swim-up bars. Being in Mexico, I thought everything would be more foreign, but in Cancun things felt a lot the same. There was McDonald's and KFC, Pizza Hut, even Wal Mart. Mel said it looked just like Florida, only more people speak Spanish in Florida.

Still, it was incredibly fun. You walk out of the hotel and down to the road, and this bus comes along. There's no schedule, because they just take you from the *zona hotelera* to the downtown. It costs fifty cents. We partied a lot because even if we got trashed it didn't matter.

There was this one club that sold drinks that were two feet tall. We'd been to Coco Bongo the night before, which was great but too crowded to dance, so we just picked this place at random because it had a dance floor. They had these long skinny glasses, red and blue plastic. I was sick of margaritas, but all you could get were margaritas and daiquiris, so I was on my third daiquiri. Usually I could drink pretty much. I started to feel kind of sick—Cancun catching up to me, I figured. I found the bathroom. I rinsed my face off, careful to keep my mouth tightly closed. I didn't want to get Montezuma's revenge.

I overheard these two girls talking. They were thin and blond, and it was clear they had never worked in McDonald's in their lives. The one was saying to the other, "I don't know if I want to come back here anymore."

The other one asked where she wanted to go instead, and they talked about Hawaii or Miami something.

I hated them. I don't know why; they were probably nice enough. But I just hated them. I thought, I almost died to get here. I still felt a little sick and dizzy, and I went in one of the stalls and sat on the edge of the toilet. Usually I don't want to touch anything in a public bathroom.

Maybe it just hit me, I don't know.

I had heard that all the guys lived, although I suspected none of them was exactly ready to come to Cancun. I had specks dancing in front of my eyes. I put my head down on my knees and took deep breaths, and I tried not to think about my head swelling up so that I couldn't open my eyes.

I'm okay, I thought. I'm okay.

Someone called, "Are you all right?" It was Mel, jingling with bracelets.

"Yeah," I said. "I'm fine."

"Are you sick?"

I was actually feeling better. I stood up and flushed the toilet and came out. "It's okay," I said. "I think I've just been drinking too fast."

The music was disco. The beat was thumping. I went out and I started dancing, too. My head was still kind of light and as I was dancing, I felt lighter and lighter. Not in a bad way, but in a good way. I thought about those girls in the bathroom. And what it would be like to be able to decide to go to Hawaii. About what it would be like to be them, or to have gotten the other kind of injection.

I thought about luck.

I could think about that, or I could dance. Right now I wanted to dance. It didn't seem like a bad choice.

The Effect of Centrifugal Forces

*When I was a kid, I had a book—I still have it, although it's in a box.
It was called* Mary Anne's Dragon, *and the cover showed a girl,
dressed for school, and in the air, coiling above her, an immense, Oriental-
looking dragon. The illustrations inside were all black and white, finely
detailed drawings; full of texture and detail that filled the page. My
favorite illustration showed Mary Anne's father, the magician, in his
study at his desk. He was young, maybe in his thirties. He had fine
black hair and a drooping black mustache and black eyes and wore a
black turtleneck, and he took Mary Anne quite seriously. You could tell
by the way he was looking out of the page that he was not patronizing.*

*I loved his study even more than I loved the magician. Behind
him were cabinets full of little drawers. They were all quite firmly
and neatly shut, but the fact that there were so many of them meant
that they had marvelous things in them. On top of the cabinets, near
the ceiling, were a glass orb that reflected Mary Anne, some plants, a
statue of a horse. The rug was an Oriental rug, and even though the
illustration was black and white, you could just tell that it was full of
colors, reds and yellows. On the magician's desk were candles and an
ink bottle and some books and a skull.*

*There was a brass orrery, a mechanical model of planets circling
the sun.*

*It was all cozy and pure and safe. I swore I would have a room
like that, but I never have. —Alice*

Maureen F. McHugh

Irene hated Alateen. For awhile, Alateen had been okay. Now, when Alice dropped Irene off for a meeting, Irene swore to herself that she would not talk during the meeting. She would remain detached.

The meeting was at a Lutheran church. The parking lot was recently resurfaced. Alice had mentioned it. "Black ice," she had said. "Skateboarders used to call it that. I love how black it is, how ... clean."

Classic Alice comment. It was a fucking parking lot. Talking to Alice was like talking to a four-year-old. She said stuff that didn't quite make sense. She would appear to be listening to you, and then she'd interrupt you because she'd noticed something or remembered something she was afraid she'd forget to tell you. She was always cutting stuff out of newspapers or printing stuff off the internet to give to Irene. She'd given Irene an article about a study that showed that the children of gay parents were actually better adjusted than average. Which just proved to Irene that this was one more thing *her* family couldn't get right because they were a fucking freak show.

The Alateen meeting was in a room that was used for Sunday school. There were coloring book pages of Noah's ark in the windows. There were a couple where the kids had stayed in the lines and drawn the boat brown, the water blue, the giraffes yellow and brown. But a lot of them were just little kid scribbles. Orange orange orange in crayon tangles.

Naomi was there, squeezed into one of the little kid chairs. Naomi didn't just have hips, she had haunches. She had long, straight black hair and glasses. She had chipped purple nail polish. She exemplified everything half-assed. She had her blue spiral-bound notebook and was writing, furious, which meant that she'd talk about her arguments with her mom again. Naomi had an unfair ratio of talking to listening. It wasn't like she had more problems than anyone. Lots of kids had really scary stories—times in homeless shelters, in foster care, parents hauled off for involuntary detox, violence. One

148

of the reasons that Irene had decided that she wasn't going to talk was because really, those were the kind of problems that deserved Alateen. Irene's mom had split up with her other mom, her *momms*, when things were just sort of crazy. Mom and Momms, together, and then Momms split and there was just Irene and Mom. It had been mostly like a normal divorce. Then Mom met Alice. Momms got, of all things, a boyfriend. *That* had been weird. The new boyfriend, Lonny, was strung out even when he wasn't necessarily high; all Adam's apple and skanky hipbones and funny nervous grin. But by then Irene had made it clear that she wasn't spending any time at Lonny's apartment, so they met at Denny's, where Momms jittered and smoothed her hair over her ear again and again and didn't eat and talked a mile a minute. Annoying, but not the same as your drunken dad punching you.

At the meeting, first they read the steps and the Serenity prayer. Then they all had to write an experience where they had gotten angry. Sandra, the meeting facilitator, gave them all little sheets of paper and pens. Naomi was the first to drop something in the bag. Something, Irene was sure, about another argument with her mother.

Irene thought about the things that had gotten her angry during the week, and then thought about which ones she would be willing to actually talk about. Nothing about Alice's piles of stuff in the living and dining room of the condo. Nothing about her mother's increasing lack of coordination. Nothing about her mother and APD. Momms was a safe thing to be angry at. Momms was the drug addict, and therefore her behavior was the thing that Irene was here to talk about. Irene couldn't think of any specific thing that she'd done that had made Irene crazy, but she wrote "Momms at Denny's" on her piece of paper and folded it up and dropped it in the paper lunch bag. She used to love these exercises. But now they were just such a pain in the ass.

Irene was the last one to drop her piece of paper in the bag.

When Sandra reached into the bag, she tensed. She had promised herself she'd be silent, but already she couldn't help planning what she would say.

"Naomi," the facilitator said. "Do you want to read what you wrote?"

Fuck. Fuck fuck fuck.

Avian Prion Disease, or APD. APD is a transmissible spongiform encephalopathy (or TSE) similar in effect to Creutzfeldt-Jacob Disease (CJD), Kuru, and Fatal Familial Insomnia. Like Bovine Spongiform Encephalopathy (Mad Cow Disease), an animal-based illness that crossed from cows to humans, APD is a disease that appears to have arisen spontaneously in a chicken that was breeding stock for a large chicken producer. The resulting infection leaped the species boundary from avian to human.

The disease was spread through the food supply in processed chicken products like "nuggets." Commercial chickens are usually slaughtered within forty-two days of hatching, before they show symptoms of APD. Thus, though the disease was apparently never widespread, it was also unchecked.

In humans, APD has a latency period of about five years. No one knows how many people were exposed to the disease. The current rate of infection is about one per two hundred thousand people, but the number of cases is expected to rise over the next five or more years as APD expresses itself in people in whom it is still latent.

Initial symptoms include headaches, ataxia (loss of muscle coordination), trembling, and slurred speech. As the disease progresses, the victim becomes unable to walk without support, and the tremors become worse. The victim has wild emotional swings from despair to euphoria. In the final stages of the disease, the victim becomes incontinent and incapacitated. The victim cannot speak or swallow. The body wastes. Death occurs in six months to two years, often as a result of pneumonia or infection from pressure sores.

There is no test for the disease.

After the Alateen meeting, Irene was first into the parking lot. She really didn't feel like conversation—either the "wasn't that a great meeting" type or the "didn't that meeting suck," type. Both could come from the same person. She had engaged in both, about the same meeting, even. It pretty much summed up Alateen, except that the needle was swinging more and more into the "sucks" category and less and less into the "great." There was no sign of Alice.

Not long after Irene had started Alateen, they'd talked about cell phones in one of the meetings. It had been back when Alateen meetings were more likely to be "great." It had been a pretty good meeting, as she remembered. Some girl who was no longer coming had said that she figured this was one hour out of her life she could really dedicate to getting herself straight, and she always turned her cell phone off. Irene had thought that was cool and had made it kind of a rule. She still did it, even though the hour didn't feel nearly as dedicated. Alateen seemed like one of those things, like diets, where everything great happened at the beginning.

She dug out her phone. She had three texts from Alice.

Call me.

Your mom fell, at ER.

Your mom is ok just hurt her wrist will pick u up asap

Had her mom tripped over something in the house? One of Alice's goddamn piles of crap? Fuck a bucket but life sucked.

Because of the broken wrist they gave Natalie a prescription for hydrocodone.

Alice maneuvered her through the crowded living room, holding her elbow. Past the pile of clothes waiting to be folded on the couch, and the stacks of magazines, and the pile of empty plastic storage containers, and the box of teal dishes. The painting that Alice had brought home because the frame was good. Alice maneuvered her into the bedroom and sat her on the bed. Alice undressed her, so tenderly, so sweetly, saying over and over, "All right?"

She hurt, and the shock of the fall had further loosened her mind. Her brain was being turned to holes by prions, which she thought of as tiny wires bent like paperclips. They bumped along her neurons and made more and more paperclips, turning the cells to lace.

She could not seem to stop moaning, and sighing.

Alice put a nightgown on her. Natalie didn't ever wear a nightgown, not since she was girl. Alice had bought her nightgowns of white cotton. *Little House on the Prairie* nightgowns that hung loose around her. Alice had hung them outside to dry, because the dryer was broken. They smelled of sunlight.

Wasn't Alice here? Alice wasn't here.

She sat on the edge of the bed smelling the sunstroked cotton and wondering if she should lie down.

Alice was here. Alice had a glass of water and a pill.

There was the risk that the painkillers would launch her deeper into dementia. Already, nouns fled her. She could not seem to hold them and found herself saying to Alice, "It's started, there is water, from the sky." Alice said "rain," and the word was there. Why lose "rain" but not "sky"? Why nouns? Of course, she wasn't thinking "nouns." Just a wordless *why*. She had known about dementia once, had understood it from outside. Her grandmother had dementia, not Alzheimer's but something they couldn't give a name to, something that progressed differently, something that wasn't Parkinson's, or nutrition, or drug interaction, or even (they tested for it) syphilis. Something that took away her grandmother's mind in dribs and drabs over many years but that was, in a strange way, kindly. It didn't seem so to everyone else, of course. It was terrifying. And exhausting. The way the conversation looped around the same things. The way her grandmother explained over and over that something had happened to her sister, that her sister had fallen right down (gesturing with her hand) like that, and nobody would tell her what had happened. Nobody knew. The sister had been dead for almost forty years. Still, her grandmother didn't get angry or agitated or wander. At the beginning she had been upset. She had hid the gaps in her memory. Her driving had gotten bad, and she clung to the shoulder of the road and had once taken out a mailbox. Then her grandmother went to an assisted living place and, in some strange way, relaxed. Except for the business about the long-dead sister.

Not so for Natalie. ADP was not kind that way. It jerked her muscles and made her twitch. Walking, her leg would suddenly rise high as if she were marching, knee coming up, foot kicking out. When she tried to sleep, the twitching woke her up, again and again. Sometimes it was that sensation of falling that comes on the edge of sleep. Feelings rose in her, like flights of birds, fluttering and flinging themselves against the bones of her ribcage. Anxiety made manifest. She said she wanted to be here as long as she could for Irene and Alice, but honestly, she got so tired of the knowledge that she was going to die, of never being able to put that burden down, that she craved oblivion. She took the hydrocodone for her wrist pain. There was a reason she knew that she shouldn't take the hydrocodone, and she could see that Alice knew it, too.

Alice was giving her the pill. Was Alice trying to poison her? She could not hold on to what she saw in Alice's face. This woman she knew who suddenly seemed strange. She knew her, and she did not. She was afraid, and she tried hanging that fear on Alice's face and then on the bulky cast on her wrist, so very, very white, but the fear attached to everything and nothing.

She was lying down, and Alice was covering her with a flowered sheet. "Are you cold?" Alice asked.

She was thirsty. Her arm jerked, and her wrist throbbed. She heard herself moaning, but it didn't seem like her. She certainly had no control over it. Irene stood in the doorway, watching. She looked at Irene.

It went on and on, and Irene wasn't in the doorway anymore.

The pill tugged at her, finally, pulled her down. She closed her eyes.

It would be nice to say that she dreamed of Irene. Or that she remembered things. She had delirium dreams: the world was out there, and she could access it on a screen against her eyelids, like her smart-phone, but every time she moved her eyes, she moved to a different screen. She had made something happen in the world every time she did that, like hitting enter on a computer, and she didn't know what she was doing. She was causing trouble for everyone, but her eyes kept flicking.

This was not her. This was a remnant. A fossil.

A few weeks before, Natalie had gone out. She drove, not know-ing it was the last time she would drive, but knowing that maybe she shouldn't. She was hungry and nearby in a strip mall was a place that sold hamburgers. It wasn't a chain, and she had thought it might be better because it wasn't a place that had been made to be like other places. It was a placed that dreamed of becoming a chain. Its signa-ture, for God's sake, was a pastrami cheeseburger. It had six tables and white walls and somehow just failed being either retro or current, but at 11:30 it was half full of people. She lived a relentlessly white, liberal life just five or six blocks away, but here on Venice Boulevard, the kids eating their grilled cheese and chicken sandwiches and bacon cheeseburgers were all brown and black. (None of them had ordered the pastrami cheeseburger, and neither did she.) There were lots of places on Venice where liberal white people went. Thai restaurants, and Indian, and even Himalayan (they had yak chili on the menu), but this was not that kind of place. It turned out to be a place where the fries were made from frozen and the bun had sat in a dry steam tray long enough to get a little tough around the bottom. The kids were chattering and goofing for each other, and a sharp-faced girl was being cynical and unimpressed. They paid no attention to a lady with a cane. The guy who fried up her cheeseburger brought it out to her table instead of calling her to the counter. (He wore one of those paper hats that look like boats—retro short order.) He and Natalie were the only white people in the place and she doubted he was the kind of person who ate yak chili. Irene and her friends might "discover" this place, but they would be slumming, and that would be part of the charm. The kids here today were not slumming. They owned this place, it was in their territory, and she had passed through the semipermeable membrane of class. The burger was fresh and the fries, honestly, were better than those things they served at In-N-Out. She read her book and ate her burger carefully.

When she was finished with her burger, she sat a few minutes to finish her book. She was ignoring the beating anxiety in her chest. She was carefully not thinking about this being the last time, or about the kids with their lives in front of them, although she wanted to ask the kid who had ordered the chicken sandwich if he was crazy. But they said on the news that there was no danger from ADP in the current food supply, and anyway, all of these kids had eaten chicken nuggets in the last five years and for all any of them knew, paperclips were bumping along their neurons.

She finished her book and gathered her things, including her tray. On the TV in the corner there was a commercial for the army. This was the kind of person she had been before ADP made holes in her brain. A person who had not been made completely self-absorbed by disease, unable to think of anything but how frightened she was. A person who noticed moments like this—the joint, the commercial

There's strong. And then there's Army strong. Which seemed perfectly to suit this restaurant, to be aimed like an arrow at these kids, who were ignoring it, and to have nothing to do with Irene and her friends, who would not dream of the army. And, of course, to have nothing to do with her, who was dying, dying, dying.

Lonny drove because Eva was tweaked and why wouldn't she be since they were going to see her dying ex-girlfriend and her kid who she had no legal right to? Eva jittered and fidgeted in the passenger seat.

"Quit," he said. She was picking at her skin. She was looking bad. She needed a haircut. Frankly, she couldn't handle all the shit the world was handing her. Some people just couldn't. And it was a lot of fucking shit. "We don't have to stay long," she said.

Natalie had a house, a little ranch that must have cost a fucking mint. Eva said her parents had money, and they had made a whopping down payment. Lonny hadn't picked his parents quite so well. "Pull in the driveway," Eva said. "You can't park on the street. It's residents only."

"What the fuck?"

"You got to have a permit to park on the street," Eva said. "You can only get one if you live here. See the tags hanging off the rearview mirrors?"

"That's assholian," Lonny said.

"Don't give me a hard time!" she said. "I can't take it right now." She was all tense and rigid. She had done something with her hair a few weeks before, something that made it reddish, and it didn't do her any favors. Eva was getting hard to take. But there wasn't a whole lot he could say. What was the point? They were all going to die of APD anyway. Jesus, he'd eaten enough chicken from fast-food joints to start growing feathers. Eva was sure as shit that she had it. She was always worried she had the shakes, but that was just 'cause she was cranked half the time. He wanted to say it was okay, slow down, relax, but it wasn't okay, and it sounded like a lie when he said it. They just did what everyone else was doing, which was to pretend everything was normal.

"I didn't mean anything," he said. "I don't care. It's just stupid, you know? No skin off my back, though."

"We don't have to stay long," she said, again. Maybe she did have it. Maybe she was forgetting.

Maybe he was just freaking himself out.

Alice met them at the door. Alice was what, in her thirties, and not what he expected. She didn't look dykey or anything. Eva wasn't dyke-looking. Alice looked boring. She had blond hair out of a bottle and big hips and no makeup. Eva was so intense, so alive, he'd just assumed that Natalie would have picked someone more *there*. She looked normal, though. Irene talked about her like she was a freak, but mostly she looked like a bank teller or something.

The inside of the house was un-fucking-believable. Shit piled everywhere. Irene was right about that. The couch pulled out from the wall, and stuff and clothes piled behind it up halfway to the ceiling.

"Thanks for letting me come by," Eva said. "We won't stay long. I know it's weird, having me here and stuff. Nat's probably told you some crazy stuff. God, that birdcage is so cute, where did you find it? I've got to do something with our place; it's all Lonny's stuff, and it looks like a bachelor pad. Is Irene here?" Eva seemed unable to stop talking, and she was staring at everything. There were a ton of books. Eva had read magazines and stuff when they first met, but now she couldn't even sit still for the TV. There were stacks of books beside the chair and the couch, and the couch was covered with more clothes and bags. There were bags from Target with stuff still in them—he could see running shoes with the tags still on them. Alice didn't look like she was the kind of person who went running, and neither did Irene.

"I was going to straighten up," Alice said. "It's just hard. You know, with everything that's going on."

"Totally," Eva said. "I mean, I understand completely."

"The Home Health Aide was here earlier. She comes three times a week. But the rest of the time it's just me."

"And Irene," Eva said. "But I know you're doing the lion's share and all that."

Irene came out of her room. "Hi," she said.

"Hi, baby," Eva said.

Irene was Natalie's biological daughter. There had been some thing about Eva's brother being the sperm donor, but Eva said he had freaked out about it, and they had ended up using an anonymous donor. Irene looked a lot like Natalie. Not fat, but short-legged with thick ankles and wrists. She had longish light brown hair and brown eyes. She wasn't pretty. Mostly, when Lonny saw her, she was like this. Monosyllabic. Eva said she was smart, and ever so often she said something sharp and sarcastic, and he'd see what she might be like with her friends. She didn't like him, but that was okay; he'd never been too excited about the guy his mom lived with in Tennessee. He wondered if she was gay. Not that it was genetic or anything, but still, growing up with two moms and all that. Eva hadn't turned out to be exactly gay. *I was confused*, Eva said once, but honestly, he suspected that she really was gay but that it didn't really matter that much to her who she had sex with, exactly. Which sounded fucked up, but he didn't know any other way to think about it.

Eva headed for the bedroom and he trailed along behind, not sure if he was supposed to wait in the living room or what. There wasn't any place to sit down in the living room anyway, and the kitchen table and chairs were piled up, too.

The bedroom was crowded. One whole wall was stacked with those plastic storage containers with more piles of clothes on top of them. The other side was like a miniature hospital. He saw a package of adult diapers and averted his eyes. It smelled like a hospital, too. He wouldn't have known Natalie. She was emaciated, dressed in an old-fashioned white nightgown. Her head looked too big for her neck. Her eyes were huge.

"Hey, look who's here to see you," Alice said.

Natalie's eyes rolled toward them. She had a cast on one wrist. She tried to say something but her voice was a smear.

"She's hard to understand," Alice said. "Sometimes she's better, but she's had her antianxiety meds, and they make her slur more."

Eva was stricken. Lonny didn't blame her. This was it, the future. This was what they were all going to be. Holy fucking Christ. By the time he got it, with his luck, so many people would be sick, there wouldn't be enough people to take care of them. He figured if he got sick he would go to the VA, but really, if he got like this, he was going to OD. Take so much stuff his heart shredded.

He went back out to the living room and then, since there was no place there, out the front door to sit on the front step.

Irene came out and sat down beside him.

"Sorry," he said. The house across the street had bougainvillea blooming and a lemon tree in the side yard. California. It was unreal.

"It's okay," she said. "It's fucked up."

"It sure is," he said.

At least he'd gotten to grow up in normal times. They'd been convinced that the US was going down, that China would run the world, and there'd been 9/11 and all that, but they hadn't thought everyone was going to die except the vegetarians. Sometimes he still thought everything was going to be okay. Some people would get sick, like AIDS, but people would still go to work and stop and buy gas at $5.49 a gallon and whine about inflation, and it would be normal fucked-upedness.

"She can't eat anymore without choking," Irene said, matter-of-fact as a heart attack.

"Yeah?" he said, because what else do you say?

"They want to put a feeding tube in. But Alice and I talked about it. We don't think they should."

She sounded like a grown-up. Well, that's probably what watching your mom die horribly did to you.

"Why not?" he asked. He wasn't sure he really wanted to know, but she seemed to want to talk, and she never talked to him.

"What for?" she said. "We're going to get hospice in."

"Hospice," he said. "That's good. That's really good."

"I want to ask you something," Irene said.

"Sure," he said.

"You saw the house, right? I mean, that's crazy."

He wasn't sure what they were talking about—the stuff, the hospital room? He nodded as noncommittally as he could.

"Can I come live with you and Momms when Mom dies?"

We moved a lot. I went to seven different schools in twelve years. I wasn't an army brat. My dad went back to finish a college degree when I was five, and then he went to grad school for two years. Then they moved three times in two years because they lived with my mom's parents, then dad found a job with a nonprofit that went bust and then got work through a grant. He was a chemist working with companies that did environmental studies. Analysis of water systems. He had trouble working for other people. Every move was the last one. Every job was the good one. The last three moves were without my dad—back to my mom's parents, then to one job for my mom, and halfway through the school year, the last one. My mom is still in that house.

When my mom and dad split up, my mom made me get rid of most of my stuff. I wasn't a hoarder then, but I always had a thing about my stuff. She said we could only take what would fit in the car. I had a collection of statues of horses and some stuffed animals and some shells from a vacation in Florida. Sanibel Island, which was boring, but I loved the shells. It was my museum. My history. I could tell you when I got each horse. Each one had a name and a story. I was fifteen. We had a huge fight. We were both upset because of the divorce. Her because it was a failure, I think—a failure of a marriage and a failure of judgment. Me, because it had taken so long for her to finally do it. She threw out the horses and the stuffed animals and the shells.

It was a big deal. I was devastated. It was like she had thrown out my entire past. I realize that she didn't understand. I don't hold it against her. But it was big. Really big.

Hoarding runs in my family. My granddad is a hoarder, only they say pack rat. I haven't been there in years, but last time my mom and I were there after my grandmother died, there was this smell, like canned peas or something. Musty. I know things are too cluttered, but it's not as bad as that. It's gotten a little out of control now that Natalie is sick, I know. But I can't do anything about it right now. I can only handle so much. After Natalie is gone, I'll have to do something.

Nat's parents want to take Irene, but she needs to stay in her own house, with her friends. High school is too important a time to take her away from everything.

I don't want to. I want her to be somebody else's problem. She hates me, and I don't really like her, but when I committed to Natalie, I committed to everything that came with it. We would have gotten married if we could have. Natalie is my wife in every way that I can make it so. Irene is her child. It's not Irene's fault, she didn't pick me or my problems. She's already been abandoned by Eva. Eva chose drugs over her daughter. I owe Irene the best I can give her. I do. I want to work on that, see if we can find a way to love each other.

That's not realistic, is it? I read in a book on stepparenting that you can never replace their biological parent, but you can become someone important in their lives. That you can become an adult they can tell things they couldn't say to a parent. Like a beloved aunt or something.

I don't know that Irene and I can have that, but I feel like I have to try. She can't live with Eva. She doesn't want to go to Texas and live with her grandparents. That leaves me, right?

I know that my stuff is a problem. But it's really not that bad, not as bad as Irene makes it sound. Irene is hurt and angry and lashing out.

When Natalie is gone, then I'll concentrate on dealing with the stuff. I will. I'll work with the professional organizer you talked about. I don't want to stop seeing you and work with someone who has more experience with people like me. Will you continue therapy with me?

Those horses were worth some money. People collect them. Not that I would ever sell them if I had them again.

Everything goes away. You just try to hold on to what you can.
—Alice

Irene went through the dark house to the kitchen and got a Coke. The only light in the whole house came from her room, because then she didn't have to see anything, although the problem with that was sometimes the piles kind of slid, and something fell in the path through them, and it was easy to trip.

Alice was at the hospice with mom. Alice stayed at the hospice all the time now. She had come home Wednesday and done some laundry and taken Irene back with her. Alice slept there. Irene couldn't do that. She couldn't make herself do it. She had gone back on Thursday evening. She had said she didn't want to go tonight. She thought Alice might give her a hard time. They were pretty sure her mom was going to die in the next couple of days.

Alice said, "Let me know if you need anything."

"Can I have some money to order a pizza?"

Alice dug in her purse and handed Irene a wad of bills. It turned out to be over sixty dollars. "Call a friend if you want. Call me if you want to come to the hospice. I'll call you if anything happens."

"Happens?" Irene said, cruel. "Like she dies?"

Alice just looked at her for a moment. "I'll call you if they tell me she's going. You can come if you want."

Irene said, "She's not even really there." Her mom was gone. Just this thing with half-open eyes and a gaping mouth, breathing really loud. They had an IV in her to keep her hydrated, but they didn't even have to give her painkillers anymore because her brain had been replaced by cheese.

"I know," Alice said. "I just have to be there. But it's okay if you're not."

Alice was probably glad to get away from her.

So St. Alice was at the hospital, and Irene was drinking a Coke. Of course, Alice would have a life when Mom died. She'd be sad, Irene knew that. But Alice lived in Alice-world. Alice didn't really see all the stuff. Alice talked about whether Irene would take some classes at college next year for advanced placement, like everything would be the same. Alice didn't know that Irene had asked Lonny if she could live with him and Momms. (Lonny's face had said everything, even though he'd sort of talked around and said, sure, it was fine with him but he'd have to talk to Eva and they really didn't have much space in their place.)

Irene was pretty sure that if she moved to Momms's, Alice would barely notice.

She really didn't want to move to Momms's. Momms was high when she came to see Mom, and Lonny was a waste of oxygen. The apartment had hardly any furniture, and she'd have to sleep on the couch. She had been stupid to think about it. It was just that Momms was supposed to be her mother, and she'd kind of thought maybe Momms might get her act together when she realized that Irene needed her, really needed her.

Irene sat on the bed, crying. If Alateen had taught her anything, it should have taught her that Momms wasn't going to magically stop using and clean up her act for Irene. (Oh, God, Irene needed her to. Couldn't Momms see how bad things were? How badly Irene needed her?)

She cried for a while. Then she opened her laptop and tried to find something to watch on Netflix.

She hated Houston. She didn't know anyone there except her grandparents, who were okay but who never really accepted that Mom was gay and always did the "everything is so normal!" thing when they went to visit. She felt like a science experiment in Houston. Her grandmother took her shopping and watched what she picked, waiting to see if Irene was gay. They'd probably send her to one of those Bible places meant to cure you of being gay. Irene didn't actually think she was gay, but if she went to Houston, she'd probably turn gay just because of her grandparents.

If only she could have her old life back. Before Alice. Even without Mom, if she could have ... what?

If she could just get rid of Alice's stuff. She'd be eighteen in two and a half years. She could avoid Alice, if it wasn't for Alice's stuff.

Alice's fucking stuff.

She thought about running away. She closed her laptop and packed a few things. But it was just going through the motions. Drama.

She turned the light on in the living room and looked. In the kitchen she got some garbage bags, and she started picking up clothes and putting them in the garbage bags to throw them out. She could just throw everything out.

But if she put stuff out for the trash, for one thing there would be so much of it she didn't know if the trash people would take it. On TV when they cleaned out hoarder places, they brought big trucks to load stuff in. She could try calling one of those hoarding shows and see if she could get Alice on. "Hey, my mom is a lesbian who died of APD, and my stepmom is a hoarder!" Maybe the whole lesbian thing would get the TV people interested.

But Alice would probably have to agree, and Alice probably wouldn't.

Fuck Alice.

Fuck cleaning.

She got her backpack with her laptop and her phone. She packed a few things. She took it all outside to the front yard. It was a cool and breezy evening and from the front yard, the house looked nice and normal. Irene went to the garage, going in the side door and switching on the light. The garage didn't have enough space for a car anymore. It had boxes of stuff that Alice had brought when she moved in "to just put in here until she could sort through it." Alice did sometimes sort through stuff. She picked up stuff from a pile and looked at it and then put it on another pile.

Irene picked her away across the garage to the lawn mower. The can of gas for the mower sat next to it. She picked it up and sloshed it. It was only about half full, but she hoped that would be enough. All the newspapers and magazines and old mail would help.

She watched for neighbors, but no one saw her carrying the gas can back in the house.

She poured the gasoline on the stack of newspapers and on the clothes on the couch, and then she just tossed the can on a pile of stuff. The matches were in the kitchen drawer with the candles. The smell of gasoline was really strong. She hoped the neighbors didn't smell it.

She turned on all the lights in the house. Was there anything else she wanted? You couldn't even tell that her mom had lived here. Not really. The walls were still painted yellow, but it didn't look anything like home. Alice had completely covered up all traces of her mom. What would Momms think? Would she finally get it? Probably not. But if it couldn't be her and her mother's house anymore, it wouldn't be anyone's.

Irene lit the match and dropped it. The fumes from the gas flashed, and she jerked her arms up in front of her face. The flash was so intense she smelled burning hair and she ran.

Outside she checked her hair. She wasn't on fire or anything, but she had blisters on her arms and they hurt. God, she was stupid. She hadn't known that was going to happen. She looked back at the house. Had it gone out? Part of her kind of wanted it to have gone out, like the grill did sometimes. But not really. She wanted to see fire. She wanted to see it burn.

There was smoke, and then inside she could see the glow of the flames. Burning all of it. Burning things clean.

She wished her arms didn't hurt. If it weren't for that, it would be perfect.

After the Apocalypse

Jane puts out the sleeping bags in the backyard of the empty house by the toolshed. She has a lock and hasp and an old hand drill that they can use to lock the toolshed from the inside, but it's too hot to sleep in there, and there haven't been many people on the road. Better to sleep outside. Franny has been talking a mile a minute. Usually by the end of the day she is tired from walking—they both are—and quiet. But this afternoon she's gotten on the subject of her friend Samantha. She's musing on if Samantha has left town like they did. "They're probably still there, because they had a really nice house in, like, a low-crime area, and Samantha's father has a really good job. When you have money like that, maybe you can totally afford a security system or something. Their house has five bedrooms and the basement isn't a basement, it's a living room, because the house is kind of on a little hill, and although the front of the basement is underground, you can walk right out the back."

Jane says, "That sounds nice."

"You could see a horse farm behind them. People around them were rich, but not like, on-TV rich, exactly."

Jane puts her hands on her hips and looks down the line of backyards.

"Do you think there's anything in there?" Franny asks, meaning the house, a '60s suburban ranch. Franny is thirteen, and empty houses frighten her. But she doesn't like to be left alone, either. What she wants is for Jane to say that they can eat one of the tuna pouches.

"Come on, Franny. We're gonna run out of tuna long before we get to Canada."

"I know," Franny says sullenly.

"You can stay here."

"No, I'll go with you."

God, sometimes Jane would do anything to get five minutes away from Franny. She loves her daughter, really, but Jesus. "Come on, then," Jane says.

There is an old square concrete patio and a sliding glass door. The door is dirty. Jane cups her hand to shade her eyes and looks inside. It's dark and hard to see. No power, of course. Hasn't been power in any of the places they've passed through in more than two months. Air conditioning. And a bed with a mattress and box springs. What Jane wouldn't give for air conditioning and a bed. Clean sheets.

The neighborhood seems like a good one. Unless they find a big group to camp with, Jane gets them off the freeway at the end of the day. There was fighting in the neighborhood, and at the end of the street, several houses are burned out. Then there are lots of houses with windows smashed out. But the fighting petered out. Some of the houses are still lived in. This house had all its windows intact, but the garage door was standing open and the garage was empty except for dead leaves. Electronic garage door. The owners pulled out and left and did bother to close the door behind them. Seemed to Jane that the overgrown backyard with its toolshed would be a good place to sleep.

Jane can see her silhouette in the dirty glass, and her hair is a snarled, curly, tangled rat's nest. She runs her fingers through it, and they snag. She'll look for a scarf or something inside. She grabs the handle and yanks up, hard, trying to get the old slider off track. It takes a couple of tries, but she's had a lot of practice in the last few months.

Inside, the house is trashed. The kitchen has been turned upside-down, and silverware, utensils, drawers, broken plates, flour, and stuff are everywhere. She picks her way across, a can opener skittering under her foot with a clatter.

Franny gives a little startled shriek.

"Fuck!" Jane says. "Don't do that!" The canned food is long gone.

"I'm sorry," Franny says. "It scared me!"

"We're gonna starve to death if we don't keep scavenging," Jane says.

"I know!" Franny says.

"Do you know how fucking far it is to Canada?"

"I can't help it if it startled me!"

Maybe if she were a better cook, she'd be able to scrape up the flour and make something, but it's all mixed in with dirt and stuff, and every time she's tried to cook something over an open fire it's either been raw or black or, most often, both—blackened on the outside and raw on the inside.

Jane checks all the cupboards anyway. Sometimes people keep food in different places. Once they found one of those decorating icing tubes and wrote words on each other's hands and licked them off.

Franny screams, not a startled shriek but a real scream.

Jane whirls around, and there's a guy in the family room with a tire iron.

"What are you doing here?" he yells.

Jane grabs a can opener from the floor, one of those heavy job-bers, and wings it straight at his head. He's too slow to get out of the way, and it nails him in the forehead. Jane has winged a lot of things at boyfriends over the years. It's a skill. She throws a couple of more things from the floor, anything she can find, while the guy is yelling, "Fuck! Fuck!" and trying to ward off the barrage.

Then she and Franny are out the back door and running.

Fucking squatter! She hates squatters! If it's the homeowner they tend to make the place more like a fortress, and you can tell not to try to go in. Squatters try to keep a low profile. Franny is in front of her, running like a rabbit, and they are out the gate and headed up the suburban street. Franny knows the drill, and at the next corner she turns, but by then it's clear that no one's following them.

"Okay," Jane pants. "Okay, stop, stop."

Franny stops. She's a skinny adolescent now—she used to be chubby, but she's lean and tan with all their walking. She's wearing a pair of falling-apart pink sneakers and a tank top with oil smudges from when they had to climb over a truck tipped sideways on an overpass. She's still flat chested. Her eyes are big in her face. Jane puts her hands on her knees and draws a shuddering breath.

"We're okay," she says. It is gathering dusk in this Missouri town. In a while, streetlights will come on, unless someone has systematically shot them out. Solar power still works. "We'll wait a bit and then go back and get our stuff when it's dark."

"No!" Franny bursts into sobs. "We can't!"

Jane is at her wit's end. Rattled from the squatter. Tired of being the strong one. "We've got to! You want to lose everything we've got? You want to die? Goddamn it, Franny! I can't take this anymore!"

"That guy's there!" Franny sobs out. "We can't go back! We can't!"

"Your cell phone is there," Jane says. A mean dig. The cell phone doesn't work, of course. Even if they still somehow had service, if service actually exists, they haven't been anywhere with electricity to charge it in weeks. But Franny still carries it in the hope that she can get a charge and call her friends. Seventh graders are apparently surgically attached to their phones. Not that she acts even like a seventh grader anymore. The longer they are on the road, the younger Franny acts.

This isn't the first time that they've run into a squatter. Squatters are cowards. The guy doesn't have a gun, and he's not going to go out after dark. Franny has no spine, takes after her asshole of a father. Jane ran away from home and got all the way to Pasadena, California, when she was a year older than Franny. When she was fourteen, she was a decade older than Franny. Lived on the street for six weeks, begging spare change on the same route that the Rose Parade took. It had been scary, but it had been a blast, as well. Taught her to stand on her own two feet, which Franny wasn't going to be able to do when she was twenty. Thirty, at this rate.

"You're hungry, aren't you?" Jane said, merciless. "You want to go looking in these houses for something to eat?" Jane points around them. The houses all have their front doors broken into, open like little mouths.

Franny shakes her head.

"Stop crying. I'm going to go check some of them out. You wait here."

"Mom! Don't leave me!" Franny wails.

Jane is still shaken from the squatter. But they need food. And they need their stuff. There is seven hundred dollars sewn inside the lining of Jane's sleeping bag. And someone has to keep them alive. It's obviously going to be her.

Things didn't exactly all go at once. First there were rolling brownouts and lots of people unemployed. Jane had been making a living working at a place that sold furniture. She started as a salesperson, but she was good at helping people on what colors to buy, what things went together, what fabrics to pick for custom pieces. Eventually they made her a service associate, a person who was kind of like an interior decorator, sort of. She had an eye. She'd grown up in a nice suburb and had seen nice things. She knew what people wanted. Her boss kept telling her a little less eye makeup would be a good idea, but people liked what she suggested and recommended her to their friends even if her boss didn't like her eye makeup.

She was thinking of starting a decorating business, although she was worried that she didn't know about some of the stuff decorators did. On TV they were always tearing down walls and redoing fireplaces. So she put it off. Then there was the big Disney World attack where a kazillion people died because of a dirty bomb, and then the economy really tanked. She knew that business was dead and she was going to get laid off, but before that happened, someone torched the furniture place where she was working. Her boyfriend at the time was a cop, so he still had a job, even though half the city was unemployed. She and Franny were all right compared to a lot of people. She didn't like not having her own money, but she wasn't exactly having to call her mother in Pennsylvania and eat crow and offer to come home.

So she sat on the balcony of their condo and smoked and looked through her old decorating magazines, and Franny watched television in the room behind her. People started showing up on the sidewalks. They had trash bags full of stuff. Sometimes they were alone; sometimes there would be whole families. Sometimes they'd have cars and they'd sleep in them, but gas was getting to almost ten dollars a gallon, when the gas stations could get it. Pete, the boyfriend, told her that the cops didn't even patrol much anymore because of the gas problem. More and more of the people on the sidewalk looked to be walking.

"Where are they coming from?" Franny asked.

"Down south. Houston, El Paso, anywhere within a hundred miles of the border." Pete said. "Border's gone to shit. Mexico doesn't have food, but the drug cartels have lots of guns, and they're coming across to take what they can get. They say it's like a war zone down there."

"Why don't the police take care of them?" Franny asked.

"Well, Francisca," Pete said—he was good with Franny, Jane had to give him that—"sometimes there are just too many of them for the police down there. And they've got kinds of guns that the police aren't allowed to have."

"What about you?" Franny asked.

"It's different up here," Pete said. "That's why we've got refugees here. Because it's safe here."

"They're not *refugees*," Jane said. Refugees were, like, people in Africa. These were just regular people. Guys in T-shirts with the names of rock bands on them. Women sitting in the front seats of Taurus station wagons, doing their hair in the rearview mirrors. Kids asleep in the back seat or running up and down the street shrieking and playing. Just people.

"Well, what do you want to call them?" Pete asked.

Then the power started going out, more and more often. Pete's shifts got longer although he didn't always get paid.

There were gunshots in the street, and Pete told Jane not to sit out on the balcony. He boarded up the French doors and it was as if they were living in a cave. The refugees started thinning out. Jane rarely saw them leaving, but each day there were fewer and fewer of them on the sidewalk. Pete said they were headed north.

Then the fires started on the east side of town. The power went out and stayed out. Pete didn't come home until the next day, and he slept a couple of hours and then when back out to work. The air tasted of smoke—not the pleasant, clean smell of wood smoke, but a garbagey smoke. Franny complained that it made her sick to her stomach.

After Pete didn't come home for four days, it was pretty clear to Jane that he wasn't coming back. Jane put Franny in the car, packed everything she could think of that might be useful. They got about 120 miles away, far enough that the burning city was no longer visible, although the sunset was a vivid and blistering red. Then they ran out of gas, and there was no more to be had.

There were rumors that there was a refugee camp for homeless outside of Toronto. So they were walking to Detroit.

———

Franny says, "You can't leave me! You can't leave me!"

"Do you want to go scavenge with me?" Jane says.

Franny sobs so hard she seems to be hyperventilating. She grabs her mother's arms, unable to do anything but hold onto her. Jane peels her off, but Franny keeps grabbing, clutching, sobbing. It's making Jane crazy. Franny's fear is contagious, and if she lets it get in her, she'll be too afraid to do anything. She can feel it deep inside her, that thing that has always threatened her, to give in, to stop doing and pushing and scheming, to become like her useless, useless father puttering around the house vacantly, bottles hidden in the garage, the basement, everywhere.

"GET OFF ME!" she screams at Franny, but Franny is sobbing and clutching.

She slaps Franny. Franny throws up, precious little, water and crackers from breakfast. Then she sits down in the grass, just useless.

Jane marches off into the first house.

She's lucky. The garage is closed up and there are three cans of soup on a shelf. One of them is cream of mushroom, but luckily, Franny liked cream of mushroom when she found it before. There are also cans of tomato paste, which she ignores, and some dried pasta, but mice have gotten into it.

When she gets outside, some strange guy is standing on the sidewalk, talking to Franny, who's still sitting on the grass.

For a moment she doesn't know what to do, clutching the cans of soup against her chest. Some part of her wants to back into the house, go through the dark living room with its mauve carpeting, its shabby blue sofa, photos of school kids and a cross-stitch flower bouquet framed on the wall, back through the little dining room with its border of country geese, unchanged since the eighties. Out the back door and over the fence, an easy moment to abandon the biggest mistake of her life. She'd aborted the first pregnancy, brought home from Pasadena in shame. She'd dug her heels in on the second, it's-my-body-fuck-you.

Franny laughs. A little nervous and hiccupy from crying, but not really afraid.

"Hey," Jane yells. "Get away from my daughter!"

She strides across the yard, all motherhood and righteous fury. A skinny, dark-haired guy holds up his hands, palms out, no harm, ma'am.

"It's okay, mom," Franny says.

The guy is smiling. "We're just talking," he says. He's wearing a red plaid flannel shirt and T-shirt and shorts. He's scraggly, but who isn't.

"Who the hell are you," she says.

"My name's Nate. I'm just heading north. Was looking for a place to camp."

"He was just hanging with me until you got back," Franny says.

Nate takes them to his camp—also behind a house. He gets a little fire going, enough to heat the soup. He talks about Alabama, which is where he's coming from, although he doesn't have a Southern accent. He makes some excuse about being an army brat. Jane tries to size him up. He tells some story about when two guys stumbled on his camp north of Huntsville, when he was first on the road. About how it scared the shit out of him but about how he'd bluffed them about a buddy of his who was hunting for their dinner but would have heard the racket they made and could be drawing a bead on them right now from the trees, and about how something moved in the trees, some animal, rustling in the leaf litter, and they got spooked. He's looking at her, trying to impress her, but being polite, which is good with Franny listening. Franny is taken with him, hanging on his every word, flirting a little the way she does. In a year or two, Franny was going to be guy crazy, Jane knew.

"They didn't know anything about the woods, just two guys up from Biloxi or something, kind of guys who, you know, manage a copy store or a fast-food joint or something, thinking that now that civilization is falling apart they can be like the hero in one of their video games." He laughs. "I didn't know what was in the woods, neither. I admit I was kind of scared it was someone who was going to shoot all of us, although it was probably just a sparrow or a squirrel or something. I'm saying stuff over my shoulder to my 'buddy,' like, 'Don't shoot them or nothing. Just let them go back the way they came.'"

She's sure he's bullshitting. But she likes that he makes it funny instead of pretending he's some sort of Rambo. He doesn't offer any of his own food, she notices. But he does offer to go with them to get their stuff. Fair trade, she thinks.

He's not bad looking in a kind of skinny way. She likes them skinny. She's tired of doing it all herself.

The streetlights come on, at least some of them. Nate goes with them when they go back to get their sleeping bags and stuff. He's got a board with a bunch of nails sticking out of one end. He calls it his mace.

They are quiet, but they don't try to hide. It's hard to find the stuff in the dark, but luckily, Jane hadn't really unpacked. She and Franny, who is breathing hard, get their sleeping bags and packs. It's hard to see. The backyard is a dark tangle of shadows. She assumes it's as hard to see them from inside the house—maybe harder.

Nothing happens. She hears nothing from the house, sees nothing, although it seems as if they are all unreasonably loud gathering things up. They leave through the side gate, coming nervously to the front of the house, Nate carrying his mace and ready to strike, she and Franny with their arms full of sleeping bags. They go down the cracked driveway and out into the middle of the street, a few gutted cars still parked on either side. Then they are around the corner and it feels safe. They are all grinning and happy and soon putting the sleeping bags in Nate's little backyard camp made domestic—no, civilized—by the charred ash of the little fire.

In the morning, she leaves Nate's bedroll and gets back to sleep next to Franny before Franny wakes up.

They are walking on the freeway the next day, the three of them. They are together now, although they haven't discussed it, and Jane is relieved. People are just that much less likely to mess with a man. Overhead, three jets pass going south, visible only by their contrails. At least there are jets. American jets, she hopes.

They stop for a moment while Nate goes around a bridge abutment to pee.

"Mom," Franny says. "Do you think that someone has wrecked Pete's place?"

"I don't know," Jane says.

"What do you think happened to Pete?"

Jane is caught off guard. They left without ever explicitly discussing Pete, and Jane just thought that Franny, like her, assumed Pete was dead.

"I mean," Franny continues, "if they didn't have gas, maybe he got stuck somewhere. Or he might have gotten hurt and ended up in the hospital. Even if the hospital wasn't taking regular people, like, they'd take cops. Because they think of cops as one of their own." Franny is in her adult-to-adult mode, explaining the world to her mother. "They stick together. Cops and firemen and nurses."

Jane isn't sure she knows what Franny is talking about. Normally she'd tell Franny as much. But this isn't a conversation she knows how to have. Nate comes around the abutment, adjusting himself a bit, and it is understood that the subject is closed.

"Okay," he says. "How far to Wallyworld?" Fanny giggles.

Water is their biggest problem. It's hard to find, and when they do find it, either from a pond or, very rarely, from a place where it hasn't all been looted, it's heavy. Thank God Nate is pretty good at making a fire. He has six disposable lighters that he got from a gas station, and when they find a pond, they boil it. Somewhere Jane thinks she heard that they should boil it for eighteen minutes. Basically they just boil the heck out of it. Pond water tastes terrible, but they are always thirsty. Franny whines. Jane is afraid that Nate will get tired of it and leave, but apparently as long as she crawls over to his bedroll every night, he's not going to.

Jane waits until she can tell Franny is asleep. It's a difficult wait. They are usually so tired it is all she can do to keep from nodding off. But she is afraid to lose Nate.

At first she liked that at night he never made a move on her. She always initiates. It made things easier all around. But now he does this thing where she crawls over and he's pretending to be asleep. Or is asleep, the bastard, because he doesn't have to stay awake. She puts her hand on his chest, and then down his pants, getting him hard and ready. She unzips his shorts, and still he doesn't do anything. She grinds on him for a while, and only then does he pull his shorts and underwear down and let her ride him until he comes. Then she climbs off him. Sometimes he might say, "Thanks, Babe." Mostly he says nothing and she crawls back next to Franny feeling as if she just paid the rent. She has never given anyone sex for money. She keeps telling herself that this night she won't do it. See what he does. Hell, if he leaves them, he leaves them. But then she lies there, waiting for Franny to go to sleep.

Sometimes she knows Franny is awake when she crawls back. Franny never says anything, and unless the moon is up, it is usually too dark to see if her eyes are open. It is just one more weird thing, no weirder than walking up the highway, or getting off the highway in some small town and bartering with some old guy to take what is probably useless U.S. currency for well water. No weirder than no school. No weirder than no baths, no clothes, no nothing.

Jane decides she's not going to do it the next night. But she knows she will lie there, anxious, and probably crawl over to Nate.

They are walking, one morning, while the sky is still blue and darkening near the horizon. By midday the sky will be white and the heat will be flattening. Franny asks Nate, "Have you ever been in love?"

"God, Franny," Jane says.

Nate laughs. "Maybe. Have you?"

Franny looks irritable. "I'm in eighth grade," she says. "And I'm not one of those girls with boobs, so I'm thinking, no."

Jane wants her to shut up, but Nate says, "What kind of guy would you fall in love with?"

Franny looks a little sideways at him and then looks straight ahead. She has the most perfect skin, even after all this time in the sun. Skin like that is wasted on kids. Her look says, "Someone like you, stupid." "I don't know," Franny says. "Someone who knows how to do things. You know, when you need them."

"What kind of things?" Nate asks. He's really interested. Well, fuck, there's not a lot interesting on a freeway except other people walking and abandoned cars. They are passing a Sienna with a flat tire and all its doors open.

Franny gestures toward it. "Like fix a car. And I'd like him to be cute, too." Matter of fact. Serious as a church.

Nate laughs. "Competent and cute."

"Yeah," Franny says. "Competent and cute."

"Maybe you should be the one who knows how to fix a car," Jane says.

"But I don't," Franny points out reasonably. "I mean maybe, someday, I could learn. But right now, I don't."

"Maybe you'll meet someone in Canada," Nate says. "Canadian guys are supposed to be able to do things like fix a car or fish or hunt moose."

"Canadian guys are different than American guys?" Franny asks.

"Yeah," Nate says. "You know, all flannel shirts and Canadian beer and stuff."

"You wear a flannel shirt."

"I'd really like a Canadian beer about now," Nate says. "But I'm not Canadian."

Off the road to the right is a gas station/convenience store. They almost always check them. There's not much likelihood of finding anything in the place, because the wire fence that borders the highway has been trampled here so people can get over it, which suggests that the place has long since been looted. But you never know what someone might have left behind. Nate lopes off across the high grass.

"Mom," Franny says, "carry my backpack, okay?" She shrugs it off and runs. Amazing that she has the energy to run. Jane picks up Franny's backpack, irritated, and follows. Nate and Franny disappear into the darkness inside.

She follows them in. "Franny, I'm not hauling your pack anymore."

There are some guys already in the place, and there is something about them, hard and well fed, that signals they are different. Or maybe it is just the instincts of a prey animal in the presence of predators.

"So what's in that pack?" one of them asks. He's sitting on the counter at the cash register window, smoking a cigarette. She hasn't had a cigarette in weeks. Her whole body simultaneously leans toward the cigarette and yet magnifies everything in the room. A room full of men, all of them staring.

She just keeps acting like nothing is wrong, because she doesn't know what else to do. "Dirty blankets, mostly," she says. "I have to carry most of the crap."

One of the men is wearing a grimy hoodie. Hispanic yard workers do that sometimes. It must help in the sun. These men are all

Anglos, and there are fewer of them than she first thought. Five. Two of them are sitting on the floor, their backs against an empty dead ice cream cooler, their legs stretched out in front of them. Everyone on the road is dirty, but they are dirty and hard. Physical. A couple of them grin, feral flickers passing between them like glances. There is understanding in the room, shared purpose. She has the sense that she cannot let on that she senses anything, because the only thing holding them off is the pretense that everything is normal. "Not that we really need blankets in this weather," she says. "I would kill for a functioning Holiday Inn."

"Hah," the one by the cash register says. A bark. Amused.

Nate is carefully still. He is searching, eyes going from man to man. Franny looks as if she is about to cry.

It is only a matter of time. They will be on her. Should she play up to the man at the cash register? If she tries to flirt, will it release the rising tension in the room, allow them to spring on all of them? Will they kill Nate? What will they do to Franny? Or can she use her sex as currency. Go willingly. She does not feel as if they care if she goes willingly or not. They know there is nothing to stop them.

"There's no beer here, is there," she says. She can hear her voice failing.

"Nope," says the man sitting at the cash register.

"What's your name?" she asks.

It's the wrong thing to say. He slides off the counter. Most of the men are smiling one.

Nate says, "Stav?"

One of the guys on the floor looks up. His eyes narrow.

Nate says, "Hey, Stav."

"Hi," the guy says cautiously.

"You remember me," Nate says. "Nick. From the Blue Moon Inn."

Nothing. Stav's face is blank. But another guy, the one in the hoodie, says, "Speedy Nick!"

Stav grins. "Speedy Nick! Fuck! Your hair's not blond anymore!"

Nate says, "Yeah, well, you know, upkeep is tough on the road." He jerks a thumb at Jane. "This is my sister, Janey. My niece, Franny. I'm taking 'em up to Toronto. There's supposed to be a place up there."

"I heard about that," the guy in the hoodie says. "Some kind of camp."

"Ben, right?" Nate says.

"Yeah," the guy says.

The guy who was sitting on the counter is standing now, cigarette still smoldering. He wants it, doesn't want everybody to get all friendly. But the moment is shifting away from him.

"We found some distilled water," Stav says. "Tastes like shit but you can have it if you want."

Jane doesn't ask him why he told her his name was Nate. For all she knows, "Nate" is his name and "Nick" is the lie.

They walk each day. Each night she goes to his bedroll. She owes him. Part of her wonders is maybe he's gay? Maybe he has to lie there and fantasize she's a guy or something. She doesn't know.

They are passing by water. They have some, so there is no reason to stop. There's an egret standing in the water, white as anything she has seen since this started, immaculately clean. Oblivious to their passing. Oblivious to the passing of everything. This is all good for the egrets. Jane hasn't had a drink since they started for Canada. She can't think of a time since she was sixteen or so that she went so long without one. She wants to get dressed up and go out someplace and have a good time and not think about anything, because the bad thing about not having a drink is that she thinks all the time and, fuck, there's nothing in her life right now she really wants to think about. Especially not Canada, which she is deeply but silently certain is only a rumor. Not the country, she doesn't think it doesn't exist, but the camp. It is a mirage. A shimmer on the horizon. Something to go toward but which isn't really there.

Or maybe they're the rumors. The three of them. Rumors of things gone wrong.

At a rest stop in the middle of nowhere they come across an encampment. A huge number of people, camped under tarps, pieces of plastic, and tatters, and astonishingly, a convoy of military trucks and jeeps including a couple of fuel trucks and a couple of water trucks. Kids stop and watch as they walk in and then go back to chasing each other around picnic tables. The two groups are clearly separate. The military men have control of all the asphalt and one end of the picnic area. They stand around or lounge at picnic tables. They look so equipped, from hats to combat boots. They look so clean. So much like the world Jane has put mostly out of her mind. They awake in her the longing that she has put down. The longing to be clean. To have walls. Electric lights. Plumbing. To have order.

The rest look like refugees, the word she denied on the sidewalks outside the condo. Dirty people in T-shirts with bundles and plastic grocery bags and even a couple of suitcases. She has seen people like this as they walked. Walked past them sitting by the side of the road. Sat by the side of the road as others walked past them. But to see them all together like this ... this is what it will be like in Canada? A camp full of people with bags of wretched clothes waiting for someone to give them something to eat? A toddler with no pants and curly hair watches solemnly like one of those children in those "save a child" commercials. He's just as dirty. His hair is blond.

She rejects it. Rejects it all so viscerally that she stops and for a moment can't walk to the people in the rest stop. She doesn't know if she would have walked past, or if she would have turned around, or if she would have struck off across the country. It doesn't matter what she would have done, because Nate and Franny walk right on up the exit ramp. Franny's tank top is bright, insistent pink under its filth and her shorts have a tear in them, and her legs are brown and skinny and she could be a child on a news channel after a hurricane or an earthquake, clad in the loud synthetic colors so at odds with the dirt or ash that coats her. Plastic and synthetics are the indestructibles left to the survivors.

Jane is ashamed. She wants to explain that she's not like this. She wants to say, she's an American. By which she means she belongs to the military side, although she has never been interested in the military, never particularly liked soldiers.

If she could call her parents in Pennsylvania. Get a phone from one of the soldiers. Surrender. You were right, Mom. I should have straightened up and flown right. I should have worried more about school. I should have done it your way. I'm sorry. Can we come home?

Would her parents still be there? Do the phones work just north of Philadelphia? It has not until this moment occurred to her that it is all gone.

She sticks her fist in her mouth to keep from crying out, sick with understanding. It is all gone. She has thought herself all brave and realistic, getting Franny to Canada, but somehow she didn't until this moment realize that it all might be gone. That there might be nowhere for her where the electricity is still on and there are still carpets on the hardwood floors and someone still cares about damask.

Nate has finally noticed that she isn't with them and he looks back, frowning at her. *What's wrong?* his expression says. She limps after them, defeated.

Nate walks up to a group of people camped around and under a stone picnic table. "Are they giving out water?" he asks, meaning the military.

"Yeah," says a guy in a Cowboys football jersey. "If you go ask, they'll give you water."

"Food?"

"They say tonight."

All the shade is taken. Nate takes their water bottles—a couple of two-liters and a plastic gallon milk jug. "You guys wait, and I'll get us some water," he says.

Jane doesn't like being near these people, so she walks back to a wire fence at the back of the rest area and sits down. She puts her arms on her knees and puts her head down. She is looking at the grass.

"Mom?" Franny says.

Jane doesn't answer.

"Mom? Are you okay?" After a moment more. "Are you crying?"

"I'm just tired," June says to the grass.

Franny doesn't say anything after that.

Nate comes back with all the bottles filled. Jane hears him coming and hears Franny say, "Oh, wow. I'm so thirsty."

Nate nudges her arm with a bottle. "Hey, Babe. Have some."

She takes a two-liter from him and drinks some. It's got a flat, faintly metal/chemical taste. She gets a big drink and feels a little better. "I'll be back," she says. She walks to the shelter where the bathrooms are.

"You don't want to go in there," a black man says to her. The whites of his eyes are yellow.

She ignores him and pushes in the door. Inside, the smell is excruciating, and the sinks are all stopped and full of trash. There is some light from windows up near the ceiling. She looks at herself in the dim mirror. She pours a little water into her hand and scrubs at her face. There is a little bit of paper towel left on a roll, and she peels it off and cleans her face and her hands, using every bit of the scrap of paper towel. She wets her hair and combs her fingers through it, working the tangles for a long time until it is still curly but not the rat's nest it was. She is so careful with the water. Even so, she uses every bit of it on her face and arms and hair. She would kill for a little lipstick. For a comb. Anything. At least she has water.

She is cute. The sun hasn't been too hard on her. She practices smiling.

When she comes out of the bathroom, the air is so sweet. The sunlight is blinding.

She walks over to the soldiers and smiles. "Can I get some more water, please?"

There are three of them at the water truck. One of them is a blond-haired boy with a brick-red complexion. "You sure can," he says, smiling back at her.

She stands, one foot thrust out in front of her like a ballerina, back a little arched. "You're sweet," she says. "Where are you from?"

"We're all stationed at Fort Hood," he says. "Down in Texas. But we've been up north for a couple of months."

"How are things up north?" she asks.

"Crazy," he says. "But not as crazy as they are in Texas, I guess."

She has no plan. She is just moving with the moment. Drawn like a moth.

He gets her water. All three of them are smiling at her.

"How long are you here?" she asks. "Are you like a way station or something?"

One of the others, a skinny Chicano, laughs. "Oh, no. We're here tonight and then headed west."

"I used to live in California," she says. "In Pasadena. Where the Rose Parade is. I used to walk down that street where the cameras are every day."

The blond glances around. "Look, we aren't supposed to be talking too much right now. But later on, when it gets dark, you should come back over here and talk to us some more."

"Mom!" Franny says when she gets back to the fence, "You're all cleaned up!"

"Nice, Babe," Nate says. He's frowning a little.

"Can I get cleaned up?" Franny asks.

"The bathroom smells really bad," Jane says. "I don't think you want to go in there." But she digs her other T-shirt out of her backpack and wets it and washes Franny's face. The girl is never going to be pretty, but now that she's not chubby, she's got a cute thing going on. She's got the sense to work it, or will learn it. "You're a girl that the boys are going to look at," Jane says to her.

Franny smiles, delighted.

"Don't you think?" Jane says to Nate. "She's got that thing, that sparkle, doesn't she?"

"She sure does," Nate says.

They nap in the grass until the sun starts to go down, and then the soldiers line everyone up and hand out MREs. Nate gets Beef Ravioli, and Jane gets Sloppy Joe. Franny gets Lemon Pepper Tuna and looks ready to cry, but Jane offers to trade with her. The meals are positive cornucopias—a side dish, a little packet of candy, peanut butter and crackers, fruit punch powder. Everybody has different things, and Jane makes everybody give everyone else a taste.

Nate keeps looking at her oddly. "You're in a great mood."

"It's like a party," she says

Jane and Franny are really pleased by the moist towelette. Franny carefully saves her plastic fork, knife, and spoon. "Was your tuna okay?" she asks. She is feeling guilty now that the food is gone.

"It was good," Jane says. "And all the other stuff made it really special. And I got the best dessert."

The night comes down. Before they got on the road, Jane didn't know how dark night was. Without electric lights it is cripplingly dark. But the soldiers have lights.

Jane says, "I'm going to go see if I can find out about the camp."

"I'll go with you," Nate says.

"No," Jane says. "They talk to a girl more than they'll talk to a guy. You keep Franny company."

She scouts around the edge of the light until she sees the blond soldier. He says, "There you are!"

"Here I am!" she says.

They are standing around a truck where they'll sleep this night, shooting the shit. The blond soldier boosts her into the truck, into the darkness. "So you aren't so conspicuous," he says, grinning.

Two of the men standing and talking aren't wearing uniforms. It takes her a while to figure out that they're civilian contractors. They aren't soldiers. They are technicians, nothing like the soldiers. They are softer, easier in their polo shirts and khaki pants. The soldiers are too sure in their uniforms, but the contractors, they're used to getting the leftovers. They're *grateful*. They have a truck of their own, a white pickup truck that travels with the convoy. They do something with satellite tracking, but Jane doesn't really care what they do.

It takes a lot of careful maneuvering, but one of them finally whispers to her, "We've got some beer in our truck."

The blond soldier looks hurt by her defection.

She stays out of sight in the morning, crouched among the equipment in the back of the pickup truck. The soldiers hand out MREs. Ted, one of the contractors, smuggles her one.

She thinks of Franny. Nate will keep an eye on her. Jane was only a year older than Franny when she lit out for California the first time. For a second she pictures Franny's face as the convoy pulls out.

Then she doesn't think of Franny.

She doesn't know where she is going. She is in motion.

Acknowledgments

I will forget to thank someone. I always do. Please, I beg forgiveness in advance.

First, thanks to the folks at the Rio Hondo workshop: many of these stories were critiqued at 9,000 feet in the Taos Ski Valley. I can't thank all of you because I will forget someone, I know but thanks especially to Walter Jon Williams who first brought me to a part of the country I love more than I can say. To L. Timmi Duchamp, and to Ellen Datlow, who asked for stories. To Caroline Spector, who read for me. To the group in Austin—Jessica Reisman, Caroline Yoachim, Ellen Van Hensbergen, Jen Volant, and Meg McCarron—reading, food, and cocktails. Thanks to the folks at WisCon for making the space in the world that they do. To Karen Joy Fowler for writing what she writes as much as for her insightful comments. To Gavin J. Grant and Kelly Link for being so enthusiastic about, of all things, another collection of short stories. To Jackie Tunure at Fourth Wall Studios, who read for me in Los Angeles. To all the people I met at Clarion who have started out as students and gone on to be come friends and colleagues—you have no idea how much you have taught me.

To Adam who asked me to write "The Naturalist" based on a dream he had, and to Bob, who has always treated me as if there was nothing at all strange about my choice of careers.

Publication History

These stories were originally published as follows:

"The Naturalist" *Subterranean Online*, spring 2010

"Special Economics," *The Del Rey Book of Science Fiction and Fantasy*, May 2008

"Useless Things," *Eclipse Three: New Science Fiction and Fantasy*, October 2009

"The Lost Boy: A Reporter at Large," *Eclipse One*, October 2007

"The Kingdom of the Blind," *Plugged In*, May 2008

"Going to France," *Lady Churchill's Rosebud Wristlet* 22, June 2008

"Honeymoon," "After the Apocalypse," and "The Effect of Centrifugal Forces" appear here for the first time.

About the Author

Maureen F. McHugh has lived in NYC; Shijiazhuang, China; Ohio; and Austin, Texas; and now lives in Los Angeles. She is the author of a collection, *Mothers & Other Monsters* (Story Prize finalist), and four novels, including *China Mountain Zhang* (Tiptree Award winner) and *Nekropolis* (a *New York Times* Editor's Choice). McHugh has also worked on alternate-reality games for Halo 2, The Watchmen, and Nine Inch Nails, among others.